VENTURE SCIENCE FICTION SERIES

Series editors, Rog Peyton and Rod Milner

VENTURE
SCIENCE FICTION

ASSAULT ON THE GODS

Stephen Goldin

LEGEND

A Legend Book

Published by Arrow Books Limited
62–65 Chandos Place, London WC2N 4NW

An imprint of Century Hutchinson Limited

London Melbourne Sydney Auckland
Johannesburg and agencies throughout
the world

First published in Great Britain 1987

Printed and bound in Great Britain by
Anchor Brendon Limited, Tiptree, Essex

ISBN 0 09 952770 7

dedicated to Dorothy Fontana, for reasons that would take another book to enumerate

"I hope, for His sake, that God does not exist—because if He does, He has an awful lot to answer for."

—Philip K. Dick

1

"Just as a child needs its parents, so does an immature society need its gods. Freedom is always hard to bear, and the weight of self-responsibility can only be carried after a certain level of sophistication has been attained."
—Anthropos, *The Godhood of Man*

The road, if such it could be called, was a simple track along which the local equivalent of horses—six-legged beasts called *daryeks*—could pull rickety wooden carts. The ruts worn by wagon wheels were several centimeters deep in water, while the rest of the road was mud. There was no traffic at night, though, so Ardeva Korrell had the trail entirely to herself. The planet Dascham had no moon and the overcast sky blocked out the stars, so her universe was a darkness broken only by the light of the small electric lantern she carried as she trudged along on foot.

"In the ideal world," she mused to no one in particular, "a spaceship captain would not have to serve as her own shore patrol as well." And she sighed. Dascham was about as far from the ideal world as she ever hoped to get. She might as well be wishing for a ship of her very own, a competent crew, and the respect due her rank and experience. They were all equally distant from reality.

The dark clouds overhead threatened rain momentarily. That was not unexpected; it rained every night in the inhabited parts of this planet. The clouds were accompanied by a biting wind that chilled her spirit, despite the spacer uniform that insulated all but her head.

"I hope Dunnis and Zhurat are drunk," she said. "It will give me such pleasure tomorrow to yell into their hung-over ears and give them penalty duty." The thought warmed her for a moment, then died as her religious training came to the fore. " 'Vengeance eases frustrations only in the insecure mind,' " she quoted. " 'Sanity does not require the evening of natural imbalances.' I know, I know. But I sometimes think life would be a lot more fun if I were a little less sane."

She thought of her warm, if cramped, cabin back aboard *Foxfire*, and about the microspools that were waiting for her there. This slogging through mud toward a shanty town to retrieve two drunken crewmen was not her idea of a pleasant way to spend a cold, damp night on an alien world. But it was necessary. She'd told them she wanted them back in four hours; when six had gone by without their return, she knew she'd have to take disciplinary action. Being a female captain put her in a precarious enough position without letting the crew take advantage of her.

At least she wouldn't have to walk back. The Daschamese had generously provided the ship with a small cart for transportation to and from the village, but the two errant crew members had taken it with them into town. The only other transportation short of shanks' mare was *Foxfire*'s lifeboat, and using it for a two-kilometer jaunt was impractical.

So she walked, with mud sucking at her boots as she lifted each foot, thinking alternately about her bed and microspools aboard ship and about what she could do to Dunnis and Zhurat if she were a less-sane, vengeance-seeking person.

She came upon the town suddenly. One moment the glow of the lantern showed nothing around her but open fields, and the next she was almost surrounded by the crude hovels that served the Daschamese as houses. The ground underfoot was no better for being within the village, however; if anything, it was even more churned up from the volume of traffic that crossed over it daily.

To Dev, the settlement looked haphazard, squalid, and depressingly medieval—in short, identical to the three others she'd seen since *Foxfire* arrived on Dascham a week ago. Houses were scarcely more than huts, made out of a reedy material resembling bamboo; large chinks in the walls were filled in with mud—hardly the warmest possible arrangement. Little wonder, then, that the Daschamese wore heavy, coarse clothing; something had to be done to keep pneumonia from wiping out the race. The roofs were thatched with what appeared to be twigs, and probably only kept out 95 per cent of the water. Dev wondered whether the Daschamese would die if moved to a temperate climate; even their broad, flat feet seemed adapted to walking in mud.

Dev shook her head. It depressed her to see intelligent beings living in such physical poverty. Something was missing from their racial character, a sense of pride and accomplishment. Probably it was due to those gods they worshiped; the religious taboos were so strict that they barely allowed the people a subsistence living. "Gods fit the minds of those who serve them," Anthropos had once observed. It made her wonder about the health of the Daschamese intellect.

The village was dark and preternaturally quiet. Dev estimated the population at several thousand, yet after dark there was little indication that the region was even inhabited. It was the gods again, naturally—strict taboos against being outside after dark unless the situation was unavoidable. To be sure, even the dismal Daschamese had their night life, but it was a pale pleasure compared to those of human civilization.

It was a rule of the Universe that warm-blooded, protoplasmic creatures could be affected by fermented beverages. It was also a rule that intelligent minds often sought relief from oppressive realities by indulging in some form of mind-alteration. The combination of those two rules meant that there would be the equivalent of a bar on any world a human being could tolerate.

The Daschamese bars were built in the same architectural style—or lack thereof—as the houses, only slightly bigger. They would be lit at night, in contrast to the darkened sleeping hovels, and they would also tend to be slightly noisier—though from what Dev had seen of the natives, she wagered that the Daschamese were quiet drunks. The bars seemed to be the only places on the entire planet offering respite from the dreariness of Daschamese living . . . and it would be in one of these bars that she would most likely find Dunnis and Zhurat.

There were no streets in the village. Huts were built wherever the owners felt they were convenient, which meant that a resident had to find his way about by instinct. Dev slogged through the mire, searching the random town for her two crewmen.

It began to drizzle before she found even the first bar—a monotonous heavy mist that blurred the outlines of objects around her. Her close-cut brown hair got damp, plastering itself to her forehead and neck. But aside from the steaming of the rain as it hit the ground, there was no sound—no babies crying, no people talking, no pets yapping. It was as though the village crouched in fear from some nameless horror.

Finally she spotted a larger hut with lights shining between the chinks—a bar. She increased her pace to just short of a run. She didn't want to move too fast and fall in the mud; it would give those two clowns something more to laugh about if she came in in such a disgraceful condition.

Entering the bar, she blinked. The light was provided by candles in sconces around the walls and was not terribly bright; nevertheless, after being out in the pitch darkness of the Daschamese night, it took some adjusting to. Besides, there was a smoky quality to the atmosphere which Dev guessed was produced by some local drug other than alcohol. The smoke burned her eyes and made her rub away the tears with the backs of her hands.

When she could see again, she surveyed the interior. Four small tables dotted the floor, each with four chairs around it. Another, slightly longer table—more like a workbench than a bar—was where the proprietor stood. The floor was bare wood and the walls—except for the sconces and some blankets to cover the larger chinks—were devoid of decoration.

There were about a dozen Daschamese seated at the tables. Dev's hundred and eighty centimeter height towered over the natives, who only averaged a hundred and fifty-five. The Daschamese looked like nothing so much as animated Teddy Bears. Their bodies were covered with thick, matted fur of varying colors, they walked on broad, flat feet, and they wore heavy woolen clothes. Their short, stubby hands each contained three fingers and an opposable thumb. It was impossible for a human to read any expression in the ursine faces, but their eyes lacked the vibrant luster of the truly alive.

At the sight of her, the natives rose quickly to their feet—whether out of respect or fear, Dev couldn't say. Probably a little of each, she supposed. After all, she was one of those strange beings from the sky. Many of the Daschamese may never have seen a human close up—their planet was well outside the normal trading routes, and few ships ever ventured here. To the locals, with their primitive technology, humans must seem almost as powerful as their own gods.

Reaching up to her cheek, she switched on her translator. This was a headset with a built-in minicomputer that would translate her words into the native language as well as interpret what was said to her. "Please don't be startled," she said into the mouthpiece, and heard her own voice coming out of it in the growly Daschamese tongue. "I am merely looking for two of my friends. Have any of you seen them?"

Silence for a moment, then low growls which the computer informed her was a chorus of noes. She thanked the people and, with a sigh, ventured outside once more.

The drizzle had become a downpour in just the short time she'd been inside the bar. Dev wished she'd been able to bring her helmet with her, but she would have had to bring some oxygen tanks along in that case, and *Foxfire*'s stores could ill afford that expenditure. So her brown hair turned stringy and water dripped down the back of her neck as she trudged wearily through the darkened village to find the next bar.

It had been a drier, if more desperate, Captain Korrell that had walked up to the door of Elliptic Enterprises

11

two months earlier in search of a job. The planet was New Crete and the situation was critical. Her landlord had eyed her intently as she left the apartment; she could almost hear him wondering how long it would take to fumigate the place and move in a new tenant—one who paid rent when it was due. Her meager savings had all but evaporated, and the prospects of a job for a ship's captain who was both a woman and an Eoan were slim at best.

The door opened at her buzz, and she entered the outer office. She was immediately relieved to find that the surroundings weren't as bad as she'd expected. True, the office was located in the less fashionable part of town, but an effort had been made to preserve dignity and comfort. The floor was carpeted and the walls were painted a restful, pleasing blue; interesting bits of sculpture were tucked into the crannies and a pair of silver mobiles hung from the ceiling. The secretary's desk looked to be real wood and its top surface was busy but uncluttered. If nothing in the room completely matched anything else, at least some effort and pride had been spent in making it habitable. Dev had applied at some offices with bare floors and walls, and large insects crawling nonchalantly over the desktops. This was a distinct improvement.

The secretary—a pleasant, middle-aged woman—took her name, invited her to have a seat, and went into the inner office to inform the boss of Dev's arrival. There were some magazine spools and viewers on a small stand by the chair, and Dev started looking through them as she waited—at first just to keep down the jitters, but after only a minute she was absorbed in the subject. She considered it almost an intrusion when the secretary returned to tell her that Master Larramac would see her now.

She was ushered into the inner office, which was even more of a tribute to eclecticism. Larramac was obviously a collector of knickknacks, because the room was festooned with odd little gadgets: an old-time fire hydrant, an assortment of colorful rocks, a set of procelain flowerpots, and many little things that her eye did not recognize immediately. The walls were covered with posters: "Work is what you do so that some day you won't have to do it any more" and "I believe in getting into hot water—it keeps me clean." There were others, too, but Dev's eyes were drawn more to the man behind the desk.

Roscil Larramac was a tall man, several centimeters taller even than she was. He was very thin, and his body seemed composed entirely of acute angles. His clothes were of violent reds and blues, and his codpiece was just the triflest overpadded. His goatee was graying and his hair thinning out a bit—though not quite enough to justify a transplant. The shaven part front to back along the center of his scalp—an affectation indicating he hoped someday to join Society—was tattooed with a design of numbers skillfully interwoven to form an intriguing pattern. His eyes never stood still, but darted their gaze around the room as though fearful of missing some momentous event.

"You're Ardeva Korrell?" he asked as they shook hands.

"That's right."

"There aren't many female ship's captains, are there?" His speech was as quick as it was blunt. Dev didn't know whether that was a good trait or a bad one.

"There was one other beside myself in my graduating class of a hundred and ten," she answered formally. "However, there are even fewer red-haired, left-handed midgets in the profession."

"I suppose so. Where are you from?"

"Eos."

Larramac raised an eyebrow but said nothing, a gesture that made it impossible for Dev to interpret his thoughts. "And you want to be a spaceship captain."

"I *am* a captain. My credentials and licenses are all in order. What I'm looking for is a ship."

Larramac nodded. "My problem is that I've got a ship and, at the moment, no captain. Do you ask a lot of questions?"

"In what way?"

"Do you have to know every single thing that happens on board your ship?"

"It's a captain's duty to know everything that's going on. . . ."

"My last captain was fired for being too inquisitive."

". . . But there are some things that are not as important to know as others," Dev temporized quickly. Personal preferences must sometimes bow before the winds of necessity, after all. "My primary job would be to get the ship safely from one port to another. Everything that touches on that is my responsibility, from maintenance through astrogation. Other matters may be peripheral to the running of the ship, and on those I can tread most delicately."

Larramac ruminated for a moment, stroking his goatee. He reached into a pile of papers and took out a sheet that Dev recognized as the application she had submitted the week before. "According to your résumé, you've had a lot of different jobs. You haven't stayed with any ship more than a year. Why is that?"

Dev sighed. This was the question that was always asked, though the answer always seemed so obvious. "Prejudice. A lot of men don't like serving under a female captain. Those who don't mind that are uncomfortable about my being an Eoan. You'll notice if you check my references that my employers usually give me the highest recommendation. I'm a good captain who's been the victim of circumstance."

"I don't pay very much; I can't afford to. Six hundred galacs a month, plus standard benefits."

For a captain with her training and experience, that sum was laughable; unfortuantely, her financial situation was not. "I should be earning easily twice that," she said. "But business, I suppose, is tight."

"I'm hardly in the same class with Lenning Trans-Spacial or deVrie Shipping," Larramac admitted. "I go to the little planets they miss, the ones with the lower profit-to-cost ratios. I have to lick the bowl they hand to me, so to speak. I get by, and I've been able to build. The company has grown over the last couple of years, and I don't see any reason why that growth shouldn't continue. I keep people on if they can do the work, and I'm pretty good about raises. If I like the way you make the first run, we can talk about a salary increase."

Dev looked her prospective employer over. He seemed the honest sort; a bit oversincere, perhaps, a bit given to enthusiasms and brashness, but far from the worst of bosses she'd served.

"I've taken the liberty," Larramac went on, "of looking up your name on my chart."

"Chart?"

"Yes, the patterns of letters all have meanings, whether you know it or not. You've got a good name; it blends in well with everything else."

"I'm sure my parents would thank you; it was their choice," she said dryly. She wondered briefly about the sanity of someone who would chart a person's name before deciding whether to hire her. *Oh well, anyone who runs Elliptic Enterprises must have a few eccentricities.*

"There is one thing I would like to specify," she continued. "I must have complete disciplinary authority over my crew."

"Why is that?"

"For one thing, it's traditional. But more than that, the crew must know that you back me on all matters. As I've said, some men resent taking orders from a woman. Unless my word is law—enforceable law—I cannot guarantee the smooth running of the ship."

"Sounds reasonable. Have we got a deal, then?"

Dev nodded. "Deal. When do you need me?"

"*Foxfire* is due to leave in two weeks. I suppose you'll want to come down and see her firsthand before then."

Only two weeks to get to know a cargo ship from top to bottom? "Space, yes! I'd better start tomorrow getting the feel of her, learning what her capabilities and idiosyncrasies are."

Larramac looked at her strangely. "I thought you Eoans didn't swear by Space."

"Popular misconception. We aren't particularly awed by the mystic powers of the Universe, it's true; but when I'm speaking Galingua I have to make do with

15

the phrases that express my thoughts, including the conversational clichés. Ideological purity is no substitute for comprehension."

"You're a strange woman, Captain Korrell."

"I shall choose to accept that as a compliment, Master Larramac," she smiled. "Anything that isn't a direct insult is easier to accept as a compliment."

"I insist on being called Roscil."

"And personally, I prefer Dev for myself."

"Then Dev it is. Would you care to have lunch with me?"

Dev hesitated. That, though she hadn't mentioned it, was another of the reasons she had moved from job to job—overly amorous employers who thought a female captain's duties were horizontal as well as vertical. She was neither a prude nor a virgin, but she'd learned through bitter experience that sex frequently fouled up business relationships. On the other hand, her financial situation was such that no free meal could be unreasonably turned down. Larramac's bluntness was refreshing, but it could become just as obnoxious as somebody else's fanny-patting. *I suppose I'll have to find out about him sometime,* she thought. *It might as well be sooner than later.* "That sounds like a good idea," she said.

As she trudged through the Daschamese rain, Dev thought warmly of that lunch. Larramac's brash exterior might intimidate most people, but she was able to see beyond it. There was a lonely man inside there who would rather reject than be rejected. He didn't make a single pass at her that time, for which she had been grateful. He'd made one about a week later, which she had been able to fend off skillfully without hurting him. Ground rules thus established, he kept politely within them.

Of course, there were other things she could have strangled him for—such as his insistence on coming along on this first trip to "see how well you do." But despite that, she was reasonably satisfied with him.

Lights from another Daschamese bar twinkled faintly

in front of her, and she turned toward it. As she approached, she could see, standing beside the building, the cart that the Daschamese had lent the ship—a pretty fair indication that her wayward crewmen were there. She quickened her pace slightly.

The two men were easy to spot the instant she entered the bar—they were the only splash of color in the place. Gros Dunnis, the engineer, was a big, hulking male, a full two meters tall and clad in a spacer uniform of dark green and silver. His red hair and full red beard were matched, at the moment, by an almost equally red face that signaled his intoxication. Dmitor Zhurat, the robot-wrangler, was a much shorter, squatter man—in fact, he was about the same size and shape as the natives. Still, his red and blue uniform stood out easily among the drab earth colors used in the Daschamese clothing.

Zhurat was the first to spot her. "Well, if it isn't our pretty little cap'n comin' down out of her tower to join us. Gros, we have a dishtinguished visitor. We musht show her dignity."

Dunnis, a more pleasant drunk, beamed at her. "Hello, Captain, care to have a drink with us?"

"You both should have been back at the ship two and a half hours ago," Dev said evenly. "I think you'd better come along with me."

"We musht have forgotten the time," Zhurat sneered. "But join ush in a drink and then we'll go."

"You know I don't drink."

"That'sh right. You're too good to drink with ush, aren't you?"

" 'The sane mind needs no external stimuli to relax itself,' " Dev quoted.

"Are you calling me crazy?"

"I'm calling you drunk and disorderly. Your pay is going to be docked and you'll be given penalty duty. I'd advise you to come along peacefully, before there's trouble." She spread her feet slightly in a crouched state, prepared for anything.

The proprietor, over in the corner, was showing signs of agitation. He kept repeating something over and over.

Without taking her eyes off Zhurat, Dev switched on her headset translator once more. ". . . too many in here, there are too many in here," the bartender was saying.

"My friends and I will be leaving in a second," she told him.

The proprietor, though, was little comforted by her promise. He clapped his hands together several times in what Dev had come to understand was the Daschamese gesture of nervousness. "The gods will be offended, there are too many," he said.

Dev ignored him and continued speaking to Zhurat. "I'll tell you only one more time. Let's go."

"Damned shnotty Eoans," Zhurat muttered. "Think they're better'n anybody elsh. . . ."

Dev moved smoothly across the room and clamped a hand on her subordinate's shoulder. "Come on, Zhurat, it's time to go. You'll be a lot more comfortable back on the ship. We don't want to offend these people's gods. do we?"

"Let go of me!" Zhurat bellowed. He shrugged his shoulder to rid it of the captain's hand, but the fingers clamped tightly, painfully, and would not leave. He stared up at Dev's face and found it as stern as a marble statue. He looked back down quickly at his half-empty glass.

"You don't want to make anyone angry," Dev repeated in mild but firm tones. "Me or the gods."

"Gods!" Zhurat snorted. He stood up and Dev removed her hand from his shoulder. "There are no gods." He turned his own headset back to translate and repeated his remarks. "There are no gods!" he said loudly.

He staggered over to the center of the room. "You're sheep, all of you," he said. Dev assumed the computer translated "sheep" into an appropriate local reference. "You have no guts, you have no fun, you have no lives. You live in these miserable little huts because you're afraid to grab life for yourselves, and you make up these big, bad gods as an excuse so you don't have to do anything. You're frauds, all of you, and your gods are the biggest frauds of all."

The atmosphere within the room had become deathly quiet. All eyes, human and Daschamese alike, were turned on Zhurat. The silence was like the one between the last tick on a time bomb and its detonation. Dev cleared her throat. "I think you may have hurt their feelings," she said.

The remark only fed his fires, though. "I'll show you," he shouted. "I'll show you all." And he raced suddenly out of the bar.

"Come on," Dev said to Dunnis. "Help me catch him before he hurts himself."

The rain was coming down even harder as they went out after him, a cold, beating rain that dimmed the vision and pounded the head. The rhythm of the falling drops was almost enough to drown out her thoughts. Dev was disoriented, and the glow of her lantern went only a few meters before being absorbed by the blanket of darkness. Zhurat was nowhere in sight. She had no idea which way he had gone, but straight ahead seemed the best choice. She grabbed Dunnis's hand and pulled him along behind her like a little child.

Twenty meters ahead, they saw Zhurat standing alone in a small cleared space between some huts. "Come out, oh great gods," he was shouting. "Where are you? Let me see the power of the mighty gods of Dascham!"

Eyes were peeking through chinks in the huts, staring in disbelief at this strange being who challenged the gods. Was he brave, foolish, or a god himself that he could speak like this?

"I defy you!" Zhurat yelled. "I, Dmitor Zhurat, defy the gods!"

Forever after, that scene was etched in Dev's memory. Zhurat standing alone in the clearing, his arms raised to the sky, fists clenched and waving in the air. Then a deafening explosion and a quick flash, blinding in intensity. Both she and Dunnis were forced to close their eyes, but they could have sworn they heard a crackling sound and ... was that a scream over the driving of the rain? They could not say.

When they could open their eyes again, Zhurat could not be seen—only his smoldering uniform lying on the ground amid a pile of quickly dampening ashes.

2

"You can measure the immaturity of a people by the thickness of their law books."

—Anthropos, *Sanity and Society*

Dev and Dunnis stood there in the rain, unable to move for several seconds. Their eyes were fixed on the pitiful remains of what had only seconds before been their fellow crewman. The air felt charged with electricity, and a faint, disagreeable odor was wafting to their nostrils despite the downpour—the unpleasant aroma of burned flesh.

Slowly, they became aware of movement around them. Gathering in the darkness of the Daschamese night was a crowd of the natives, emerging from their huts at last to view the aftermath of the incredible scene. They were still being shy, and came only to the outermost edges of the circle of light made by Dev's lantern; all she could make out were the outlines of their pudgy bodies. They were gathered in a semicircle behind Dunnis and herself and staring, like the humans, at the smoldering remains of Dmitor Zhurat. The natives swayed back and forth on their feet ever so slightly, all to the same rhythm, and the air seemed abuzz with the sound of a humming—or chanting—from several score of ursine throats.

Dev closed her eyes and rubbed her forehead thoughtfully with her left hand. She felt dizzy and slightly nauseated, and wished more than ever that she'd been able to stay back aboard the ship reading some interesting microspool.

Wishes are good only in fairy tales, she told herself sharply. *This is real life, and you've got duties to perform. Get moving, woman.*

She was not sure how much time had elapsed since

Zhurat's death, but it could not have been more than thirty seconds. Opening her eyes again, she shook herself out of the shock paralysis and started to take a step forward when another sound reached her ears. At first it was barely audible over the chanting of the crowd around her and the pounding splash of the rain on the muddy ground, but it rapidly grew in strength until the air reverberated with its volume. It was a buzzing that was more than white noise; rather, it was the prelude to some other sound that would follow in due course.

Accompanying the buzzing was a light that softened the darkness of the Daschamese night. It came from overhead and grew brighter with each passing second. Some shining object was descending from the sky—a slow, orderly descent, designed to impress the audience with its stateliness. As the object came low enough finally to be seen through the driving rain, Dev found she had to shield her eyes from to total brilliance of the creature before her.

In shape it was just like the planet's natives, having two arms and two legs and a round, furry body with a snoutlike nose. But on its back was an enormous set of wings, which flapped gently as the creature floated in the air in front of the crowd. In size it was well over twice as big as any of the natives; Dev estimated its height at three and a half, perhaps four meters, with a total wing span that was easily five meters or more. The creature emanated a cool blue-white glow that lit the area for a radius of two dozen meters, and in one hand it held a long sword that shone with a brilliant golden gleam all its own. The creature's eyes were sunk deep into its face and glowed bright red, like two hot coals in a darkened fireplace.

An Avenging Teddy Bear, was Dev's first reaction, but the humor was dry on the inside of her mind. The being that floated in the air ten meters away and five meters above the ground was most impressive, and far from a cuddly plaything. Dev stood with her hand resting lightly at her waist—a few centimeters away

22

from the handle of her laser pistol—and waited to see what would happen next.

The glowing being turned its head so that its gaze swept over the entire throng gathered in the rain before it. Finally it opened its mouth to speak. Dev had her headset all ready to translate.

"The gods are omnipotent," growled the creature.

There was a chorus of answering growls from the crowd of Daschamese around her that Dev's computer translated as a round of *Amens*.

"The gods are everywhere," stated the glowing figure, and the crowd answered with another chorus of *Amens*.

"The gods are good," said the figure, and the response from the throng was the same. Dev decided to throw in an "Amen" of her own for good measure.

The litany over now, the shining creature began its speech. "The gods have the power of life and death over all who dwell on Dascham," it said. "The gods make the hunting good and the harvest rich, at their choosing. Or, to punish, they can blight the crops and spread plagues through the forest. As written in the ancient agreements, the gods are supreme masters of Dascham, and of all the people on it, and of all things that exist therein."

"Amen," said the crowd and, belatedly, Dev. Dunnis gave her a funny look out of the corner of his eye, but said nothing.

"The gods' rule is absolute," the giant creature went on. "The gods know all. There is no escape from their wisdom and their swift justice. There can be no opposition to their beneficient rule. Remember, all of you, the Time of the Burning, and know what retribution the gods can wreak for rebellion against their regime."

The creature fell silent for a second, and Dev almost blurted out "Amen" once more before realizing that no one else was going to say it. She stifled the word before it escaped her lips and waited silently with the rest until the angel chose to speak again.

"When these beings from the sky first came among you, we did not oppose them. Though many of you feared they were the demons we fought with long ago, the gods knew them to be mortal creatures like yourselves, capable of both good and evil. We did not object when they brought you trade and goods in exchange for your minerals. But when they bring heresy as well, the gods must act to defend the world that is rightfully theirs."

The creature ended that speech with its eyes focused directly on Dev. It was aware that she was the captain, and the person responsible for the behavior of the humans. She knew a reaction was expected of her; the fate of *Foxfire*'s trade mission here could well be hanging in the balance. Putting a lid on her emotions to prevent any nervousness from creeping into her voice, she stepped forward and addressed the divine messenger.

"Oh, holy one, listen to me," she said. Her voice took on the carefully modulated tones she usually reserved for control room emergencies. There was not a hint of sarcasm or irreverence in it. "Human beings are individuals, as are the Daschamese. The one individual, whose name was Zhurat, was a perpetual disrespecter of authority. He was also drunk tonight, as I'm sure you know. In your all-seeing wisdom, you are aware that I tried to dissuade him from his rash and heretical acts; that I was unsuccessful is my fault and my shame. You dealt with Zhurat according to your laws and your customs, as is your right. The gods are indeed masters of Dascham, and may deal with offenders as they see fit. But the gods of Dascham are noted throughout all the Galaxy for the fairness of their justice; I appeal to that justice not to condemn all humans for the transgressions of one such as Zhurat."

That last bit was a blatant lie. At least 99 per cent of the human race had never even *heard* of Dascham; and within the distinct minority that had, the gods were considered a quaint bit of folklore. But from Dev's extensive readings on the subject of religion, she knew all gods had one trait in common: they were immensely susceptible to flattery. With the situation as critical as it was, it would certainly not hurt to play to the egos of Dascham's deities.

24

As she finished speaking, she stepped back and bowed her head humbly to await the angel's reply. The glowing creature seemed to consider her words for half a minute before speaking again. "The gods are just," it announced, to a rousing chorus of *Amens*. "They have decided that Zhurat acted alone in his attempt to spread heresy among the true believers. He was punished in a fitting manner to show all doubters the efficiency of the gods. Quick death shall be the end of all who oppose the gods."

More *Amens*.

"The other humans appear innocent of the taint of this heresy. The gods have ruled that they shall live and continue with their trading mission as before—but the death of that one crewman shall serve as an example. All who oppose the gods shall die."

By this time Dev was well enough acquainted with the system to be able to lead the cry of "Amens" that went up from all the spectators.

"Great are the gods, for theirs is the power and the glory forever and ever."

"AMEN!"

With that last pronouncement, the Avenging Teddy Bear rose serenely into the sky once more, flapping its wings casually. Its sword glowed a brilliant gold as it waved the blade about in a menacing manner. Dev could not crane her head back too far to watch it ascend because the torrential rain was getting into her eyes. Instead, she looked over to where Zhurat's ashes had been. The charred uniform was buried in mire, and it was impossible to tell what was the remains of her crewman and what was the natural mud of Dascham.

Shaking her head slightly, she turned away from the sight. *They sure put on a terrific show*, she thought—but she was careful not to express that sentiment aloud.

Dev and Dunnis rode back to *Foxfire* in the little cart the natives had given them. The *daryek* that pulled it was an old and sickly looking beast, probably the one the villagers could most afford to spare. It was not at all happy about being forced to work at night, and showed its resentment by plodding along at a pace just barely faster than the humans could have managed on foot. The cart rumbled and jolted through the uneven ruts of the road in a way that seemed calculated to produce the biggest bruises on the passengers' posteriors. Still, Dev remembered the unpleasantness of her walk into town along this road, and decided that these indignities were to be preferred—barely.

The two people were silent for half the ride, contemplating all they'd seen. Finally, Dunnis let out a large sigh. "That was spooky," he said. There was no trace of drunkenness in his voice now; Zhurat's death had sobered him up quickly.

Dev smiled slightly "I can't argue with that."

"What do you suppose happened back there, anyway?"

"The gods smote Zhurat down for his blasphemy and an angel descended and told us to sin no more."

Dunnis gave her a quizzical look. "Do you really believe all that rigamarole?"

"That's the way it looked to me. I'm open to better explanations, if you have any."

"I thought you Eoans didn't believe in anything but yourselves."

"Are you trying to tell me what I believe in?" Dev was very careful how she said that; it would be all too easy to interpret her remark as sarcasm. Instead, she made sure to curl the corners of her mouth up in a grin, so that the engineer could see there was no hostile defensiveness behind her remark.

The big redhead threw up his hands. "Frankly, Captain, I don't know what to think. You were sure bowing and *amen*ing all over the place in front of that . . . that . . ."

" 'Angel' I think would be a good term. And I didn't bow once—though if everyone else around me was doing it, I would have. Politeness and common manners will always win you points, as long as they're applied correctly."

"But you gave in so easily to the thing, kissing up to it. . . ."

"My parents didn't raise me to be a lightning rod," Dev said simply.

"Yes, but . . . well, if there are gods, why are they only here on this out-of-the-way planet? Why arén't they in space or on any other worlds?"

"I can't answer that. I simply don't have enough information. They certainly don't seem to be in space, and I *know* they're not on Eos; if they were, the population would have been totally incinerated long ago. But I'm told gods work in mysterious ways. This is a big and varied universe; anything is possible."

"But . . ."

"Listen: a long time ago, a poet named Alexander Pope once remarked, 'One truth is clear: whatever is, is right.' That, ultimately, is what I believe. What is true for the rest of the Universe doesn't matter here; what's true on Dascham is that there are gods who have very amazing powers. As long as I'm here, I intend to take that fact into account before I do or say anything. I'd advise you to do the same—the gods know everything that's done and they can hear everything that's said on this world."

"But we're speaking Galingua now; surely they don't understand that."

"Don't underestimate them. I've already lost one crewman, I can't afford to lose another." And with that she stopped talking. Dunnis, realizing she intended to say no more, sat sullenly beside her and tried to peer ahead through the rain and the darkness as their *daryek* plodded wearily along.

It was a lucky thing Dev had turned on some exterior lights when she'd left the ship, or they might have gone right past it and through the fields beyond in the darkness. *Foxfire* was small for a cargo ship—being a bullet just thirty meters tall and twelve in diameter at the base—though here on Dascham it looked gigantic. But, hulking as it was compared to the small-scale buildings of this world, it could be utterly swallowed up by the total blackness of the Daschamese night.

Dev tied the tired *daryek* to one stabilizing fin of the

ship on the off-chance that the pathetic creature might attempt to wander away during what remained of the night. Then, holding the soggy spacer uniform that was all that remained of Zhurat, she followed Dunnis up the ladder and into the airlock of the ship. Once inside she continued to climb all the way to the nose, motioning silently for the engineer to follow her up. They passed the living quarters and went instead to the control room, where Dev walked resolutely to the captain's console and flipped a couple of switches. When that was done, she sighed slightly and closed her eyes. "I think we'll be all right now."

Dunnis had watched her with growing curiosity. She had, by her actions, turned on the deflector screens around the ship. "Were you worried about meteorites hitting us here?" he asked.

"No, but the screens' field should be sufficient to jam any low-power transmission coming from inside the ship. We can talk freely now."

"About what?"

"About the gods. You were right when you guessed that I didn't believe in any supernatural beings. But the fact of the matter is that there is someone—or some group of someones—running the show around here, and they're pretty powerful."

"But what do the deflector screens . . . ?"

"Let's start at the beginning," Dev said. "Assume that these gods are mortals like us, and technologically advanced over the natives. To a race as primitive as the Daschamese, the wonders of science would look like magic, and could be exploited by anyone willing to go to the effort of doing it. For instance, the gods claim to be able to hear everything that goes on all over the world. You're an engineer; how would you manage that?"

"Microphones and transmitters," the big man said slowly. "There are bugging devices so small that the natives would never notice them for what they are."

"Exactly."

"But to do that on a planetwide scale . . ."

"Forget that for the moment. Assume an unlimited expense account and talk in technological possibilities."

Dunnis grimaced. "Yeah, it's possible—but co-ordinating all the random conversations would be a beast."

"We know they can hear what is said because they obviously heard Zhurat," Dev went on, ignoring the other's comment. "We have to therefore assume the possibility that our conversations are being monitored. Why do you think I was so careful about what I said on the way back here? We weren't out of danger yet, and you kept wanting to put us right back into it. Until we could talk securely I didn't want to say anything that would make me a candidate for their ethereal target practice."

Dunnis glanced over at the control panel, where the blue light of the deflector-screens indicator was glowing coolly. "And you think they got some of their bugs in here? How?"

"I can't be certain, but we have taken on a good deal of cargo in the past week. Some of the little devils could have been slipped in there and scattered throughout the ship by now. But if they're that small, they can't be transmitting very powerfully, and the deflector screens should put out enough interference to block them."

"What about that angel? How do you explain that?"

"It was a robot," Dev said, sitting down on her acceleration couch and idly fingering Zhurat's uniform. "It would almost have to be, to glow like that. I'm told that some fish in the depths of the ocean have their own natural phosphorescence, but it's an adaptation to their environment. This angel didn't need it—nor did it need those wings."

"Then how did it fly?"

"The same way *Foxfire* does—gravitic drive. Didn't you notice how it stayed high enough and far enough away from everyone to avoid killing us all in the drive backwash? When it did flap its wings, the beats were nowhere near fast enough or strong enough to lift something that massive into the sky. And it hovered for a long time without flapping its wings at all. Given

29

the proper equipment, you could probably build one yourself in a couple of days."

The engineer nodded. "Yes, now that you explain it, everything sounds so simple. But I still can't get over the scope of the operation."

"When you want to control a planet, you have to think big," Dev pointed out.

"I suppose so," Dunnis admitted. "Well, what are we going to do about it?"

"Our first order of business is to debug our ship—assuming it's bugged in the first place. Leaving the meteor shields on all the time is a drain on our power. Is there some way you can rig up a detector to find the transmitters?"

"Right now, Captain? I haven't had any sleep since last night. . . ."

"Neither have I. As I recall, it was the fact that you and Zhurat were out later than you should have been that started this whole chain of events. I was wondering what a fit punishment would be—perhaps a further loss of sleep would be appropriate."

She didn't add that, in order to make sure he didn't slough the job off, *she* would have to lose sleep, too—and she had done nothing to deserve punishment. *The responsibility comes with the authority*, she reminded herself. *That's why you're a captain and he's only an engineer*.

Dunnis shook his head. "Even if I weren't tired, it would be awfully hard to detect them. I haven't the faintest idea what frequency they're broadcasting on, or what their signal strength is. It'd take forever."

Dev thought that over. "Then we'll have to find one first and examine it. That should give us enough clues to build something." She stood up. "The cargo hold is the most logical place to begin our search. Let's go."

Dunnis was clearly not happy about having to work when he was so tired, but it was equally clear that he respected Dev's authority. She had at least established that much in the six weeks she'd been running the ship. Zhurat had been the only one to slight her—and now he would no longer pose such a problem again.

Although his loss would mean added work for everyone, including her, she could at least thank the gods of Dascham for small favors.

The cramped living quarters of the crew were arear of the control room. Roscil Larramac would be sleeping behind one of those closed doors, and Lian Bakori, the ship's astrogator, would be in the other room. The rest of *Foxfire*'s complement consisted of robots, who had been Zhurat's responsibility; they had been switched off for the night and stored in a special room just afore of the cargo hold. A ship this size should really have had at least double that number of crew, but Roscil Larramac was a man who cut every corner he could in his efforts to make a profit; Dev had argued with him to increase the number of the crew by at least one or two people, but he had refused. Now, at their first planetary stop, they were already shorthanded.

"*Take no joy in pointing out to people when you are right*," she quoted a twenty-second-century writer named Mellers, "*lest they take joy in pointing out when you are wrong*." Nevertheless, she would have liked to have those extra crew members.

Immediately arear of the living quarters were the Commons, which included galley, mess hall, laundry, lifeboat dock, recycler, and recreation room. Then came the robot storage area and finally the cargo hold, with the engines in the rearmost part of the ship. The layout was standard for most small trading ships, and even though she'd only been aboard two months, Dev felt as though she'd lived most of her life here.

As she approached the cargo hold, Dev thought she heard a noise coming from the other side of the door. She glanced immediately at Dunnis, and the big man nodded to indicate he'd heard it, too. Slowly and silently, then, the two of them climbed the rest of the way down to the hatch of the cargo hold. Dev pulled the laser pistol from her belt and held it at the ready, motioning for Dunnis to do the same. When both were all set, she pressed the button that would make the hatch in the floor slide open.

It was dark inside the hold, the only light being what

filtered in from the corridor where they were standing. Nothing moved, nothing seemed out of place, but Dev did not relax her guard. Reaching over to the next button, she turned on the lights inside the hold.

There, behind a row of covered boxes. It was a motion, she was sure of it. Dropping carefully down through the hole in the floor, she landed on bent knees and looked over in that direction. Over the top of the boxes she could just make out a thatch of brown fur.

There was a stowaway aboard *Foxfire*.

3

"The best morality boils down to a simple respect for others."

—Anthropos, *The Godhood of Man*

Dev stood there, slightly crouched, pistol in hand, and quickly raced through her list of alternatives. She would be within her rights, as captain of this vessel, to open fire immediately on the intruder—but that course of action would be foolish in these present circumstances. Her gun's laser bolts might damage some of the merchandise that was stacked high and crowded all around her; and anyway, the natives were not likely to be heavily armed, as their technology did not extend far beyond the knife and spear stage.

The thought crossed her mind that this might not be an ordinary native, and that its appearance here might have some connection with the earlier events of the evening. Perhaps it was some spy for the gods, come to check them out personally. But she had just been positing the gods as beings with a high technical expertise; sending a native to spy for them would not be in keeping with their characters at all. Dev ruled out that possibility for now, though she kept her gun handy. It was her personal policy when dealing with any other thinking being to use physical coercion only as a last resort.

"Dunnis," she called in a low voice to the engineer who still stood in the corridor above her, looking worriedly down into the hold. "Wake Larramac and Bakori. Tell them we've got a stowaway in the hold and get them down here. I might need their help."

The big man was hesitant to leave her. "Are you sure you'll be all right by yourself there? A woman alone with an unknown intruder . . ."

Have patience with the well-meaning, she told herself sternly. *They frequently can't help themselves.* "Go. Now. That's an order."

Dunnis went.

Dev turned her full attention back to the native. It had not moved from its initial position behind that one stack of crates. Since it must be aware that she had dropped into the hold with it, it apparently was not sure she had spotted it and did not want to give itself away by further movement. Also, it would be using the silence to listen for any sounds on her part indicating motion in its direction.

Keeping the gun at the ready, Dev turned on the translator headset she still wore. "Whoever you are, I know you're here," she said in quiet, calm tones. "My name is Ardeva Korrell, and I'm the captain of this ship. What's your name?"

The other still did not move. Perhaps it thought she was bluffing, or perhaps it was too frightened. She had to allay any fears it might have.

"I mean you no ill will," she continued. "I only want to know why you chose to hide yourself aboard my vessel. I know exactly where you are, but I promise to come no closer until we talk. If you mean no harm to me, my crew, or my ship, I guarantee that no harm will come to you."

The thatch of fur that she had originally spotted vanished from sight as the native crouched even lower behind the boxes.

"Please don't try hiding, it won't do you any good. This is a small ship, and there are only so many places you can go before we find you. I realize this is a strange and frightening place for you, and that I am an unknown and hideous creature from the stars. But I have dealt fairly with your people for the two days I've been here at your village. All I ask is to know why you've come."

Her voice echoed through the large hold, but the silence returned as the last traces of her words died away. She eyed the chamber from a tactical standpoint, wondering exactly what to do if action became necessary. The hold was not heated; the cold metal walls seemed to mirror the cold, damp climate outside, and produced a chill that made her shiver, even though the fabric of her spacer uniform kept her body at the proper temperature. Boxes and crates of various sizes were stacked closely together out of a need to accommodate a large number in a small volume; the aisles between the piles of containers were necessarily narrow, and not conducive to hectic chases. She hoped it would not be necessary.

The native still made no move to show itself. *Think,* she told herself. *Try to reason out the psychology of these people. You know enough about them to make an educated guess.* "My patience is great, but it's not limitless," she said at last. "I'm starting to get a little tired of soliloquizing. If you don't answer me soon, I'll have to take more direct action."

Then an inspiration hit her. "And after we catch you, we'll throw you out of the ship to the mercy of the gods."

That last threat hit home. She heard a sound that her computer failed to translate; it seemed more like an involuntary whimper than speech. But at least it was a reaction. She was on the right track.

"I don't want to do that," she went on. "Don't force me to. Talk to me. Now."

A low, hesitant voice growled out from behind the boxes. "Do . . . do you promise you won't send me out?" translated the earphones.

"I can't promise anything, not until I know why you're here and what you intend. Tell me your story and let me decide for myself."

"I can't tell you. The gods would kill me."

A *fugitive.* Rather than being a spy for the gods, this native was running from them. It did not seem hostile or belligerent, though; Dev guessed its crime was more of a heretical nature.

"You're safe here. The gods can't hear you while you're inside the ship." She grew bold enough to take a step toward the native, and it did not move away. "Tell me why you're here and I'll see what I can do to help you."

The native straightened up slowly and looked at her. The expression on its ursine face was impossible to read, but Dev allowed herself to imagine that it looked sorrowful and pleading.

Just then a voice boomed out from the hatchway above her. "Don't worry, Dev, we're coming. We'll get it for you." There was a slight rattle and a loud thud as Roscil Larramac's tall frame dropped down to the floor beside her. "Where is it?" he asked. His words carried loudly through the hold.

The native, who had just begun to trust in Dev's calm, reasonable tones, panicked. It felt even more frightened and, as Dunnis and Bakori also dropped into the hold, it knew it had been betrayed. Turning as best it could in the narrow passageway between the two rows of boxes, the stowaway ran in the opposite direction, toward the far wall of the hold.

Dev turned on her employer, not even bothering to hold her temper in check. "You drumming idiot, why did you have to do that? I had it all ready to give itself up. I sweated blood trying to reason with it, and it was just beginning to trust me when you came dropping through the ceiling like a whole herd of quadrodons in heat. Now it's scared all over again, twice as scared, and it'll take all of us to pry it out of here. Just what in Space did you think you were doing?"

Larramac stood his ground. He was a businessman with long experience at argumentative negotiation. His technique for dealing with being yelled at was to yell back. "I thought I was rescuing you. I thought you were in trouble. I should have known an Eoan would be too proud to admit she needed help."

The one blast of anger had purged the frustrations from Dev's system. She felt guilty about her display, but only slightly. Even the Eoans recognized the cathartic effect of emotional outbursts. "*Violent emotions can cleanse the soul,*" Anthropos had said. "*Like drugs, they must be used therapeutically—but addiction must be avoided.*"

36

Calm once more, she looked at her employer with a level gaze. "We could go on blaming each other all night, but our primary concern at the moment is catching the stowaway. It's a fugitive, apparently; I suspect it did something to offend the local gods, and it wants to hide out here. At the moment it's probably just as frightened of us as it is of the gods. I don't think it could be armed with anything more serious than a knife, but a cornered person is always dangerous."

Larramac had been prepared for a shouting battle. This sudden switch in moods caught him by surprise. "What do you suggest we do?" was all he could think of to say.

"We're shorthanded enough as it is; I don't want to risk any of us getting injured trying to capture our visitor. Besides, four people probably wouldn't be enough to do the job—not as scared as that creature is right now. I think we'd better let the robots go after it."

"Four people?" Larramac blinked and looked around. "Where's Zhurat?"

"That's a long and eerie horror story," Dev said as she walked to the ladder and climbed upward to the robot storage room. After unlocking the door, she began reactivating the robots and instructing them in what to do. "The native must be taken alive and unharmed," she insisted. "Be gentle but firm. It's frightened, but its knife should be no real threat to you."

Foxfire's company contained twenty robots of the heavy-duty class. They were tall, slender cylinders massing better than a hundred kilograms apiece and vaguely humanoid in shape, but with greater strength and endurance. The robots were of limited intelligence, which was why they needed an overseer; but Dev's orders—to capture the alien intruder—had been as uncomplicated as she could make them.

Dev deployed her mechanized troops by sending four down each aisle to the far side of the hold. The robots moved slowly and with a great deal of caution; watching them put Dev in mind of medieval monks walking in time to Gregorian chants. She felt a twinge of pity for the poor frightened native who would see these hulking machines come menacingly toward it, but there was no other way. The intruder had to be captured as quickly and as safely as possible.

As the robots closed in relentlessly on their quarry, Dev told Larramac̄ and Bakori of the events that had transpired earlier that evening in the village. Both men were astonished to hear of Zhurat's death by divine lightning bolt, and of the angel's speech. Without going into too many of her suppositions about the nature of the gods, Dev told them that turning on the meteroid shields should make their conversations within the ship safe from eavesdropping.

The robots were now approaching the native at the far end of the hold. The little bearlike being knew it was trapped, but refused to give in to the overwhelming odds against it. Realizing that its knife would be ineffective against the big machines, it looked around for some other weapon to use. In desperation it picked up one large crate with both hands and flung it at the nearest robot. The machine lifted one arm to defend itself, and easily deflected the oncoming missile. The crate crashed into a stack of boxes and sent them toppling over into the next row in the path of more oncoming robots, delaying the pursuers and scattering the contents along the ground.

As the robots paused to pick up the fallen merchandise and work their way around the toppled boxes, the stowaway saw a momentary opening. Moving with a speed almost inconsistent with its round, bulky body, the native darted through the group of robots in one aisle and dodged under their wildly flailing arms. Suddenly it was behind the machines that had been trying to capture it, making a mad dash for freedom— though where it expected to go was a mystery to Dev.

For the moment, though, it was headed almost directly toward her engineer. "Dunnis!" she cried— superfluously, for the big man had already seen the native coming and was ready for it.

Dunnis had to take only three steps to his right to be in position to intercept the alien. As the furry creature came racing toward him, the redheaded engineer crouched low and spread his arms wide to gather in the fugitive. The Daschamese was so intent on escaping from the robots that it didn't even notice the human until it was only four meters away, by which time it was far too late to check its forward flight. The two beings collided with a jarring thud that Dev could feel halfway across the cargo hold.

The engineer closed his huge arms around the native, who struggled fiercely to get away. The other three humans raced over to Dunnis's aid, and Dev whistled for assistance from several of the robots, who were standing around wondering what to do. Though the alien put up a good fight, it was quickly subdued and handed over to the care of two robots.

"Take it up to Zhurat's cabin and lock it in. Then stand guard on either side of the door to make sure it doesn't get away," Dev ordered the machines. "We've got to get this mess tidied up here before we can question it further."

As the robots moved to obey, she glanced around at the chaos in the hold. Altogether several dozen large boxes had been knocked out of their neat stacks and lay shattered on the floor. Dev noted with interest that this was a section of the hold that had been kept a mystery to her; Larramac had refused to say what was in those particular crates and what planet they were intended for. Dev had not pressed the matter too carefully, mindful of how her predecessor had lost his job; but now it would be impossible for her boss to keep her from finding out the secret of their cargo.

As she walked over to the spilled merchandise, she had to make a conscious effort to keep her surprise under control. The floor was strewn with weapons of all sorts, ranging from laser pistols to rifles, grenades, automatic weapons that could level villages—enough lethal equipment to stock a small army. And that was only in the crates that had broken open. How much more of an arsenal was still in the sealed containers?

Roscil Larramac was a gunrunner.

* * *

Though Larramac knew she had seen the cargo, neither of them said a thing about it. Dev had several other problems requiring her more immediate attention, and she preferred the luxury of working on one at a time. The matter of the guns was filed in the back of her mind for future comment—but it was far from forgotten.

"Can you three men direct the robots in the clean-up?" she asked Larramac. "I figured that, since I began talking to our captive before, I might as well continue the job. If you have no objections."

"No, no, go right ahead. We'll take care of things down here, if you're sure you'll be all right upstairs." The ship's owner talked quickly, trying to cover some latent guilts about the cargo.

Dev willingly left the house cleaning to the men and machines as she climbed up through the central core of the ship to the level of the crew's quarters. As per her instructions, Zhurat's room was locked and a robot stood on either side of the door.

"I'm going inside there," she told the two robot guards. "If the alien tries to escape, grab it and hold it—but don't hurt it." And with that, she unlocked the door and entered.

The alien sat on the fold-down cot at the far end of the small cabin, cowering against the bulkhead and glaring at her intently. From the style of clothing and the general body structure, she concluded that her captive was a male of his species.

"Hello again," she said calmly, closing the door behind her and leaning casually against it to give subtle reinforcement to the concept that he was her prisoner. Her pistol was set in its holster now; her hands were empty and spread apart in a gesture of peace. "Despite all the excitement of the last half hour, nothing really has changed. We still mean you no harm. We could have killed you by now, but we didn't. That should prove some of our good intentions. Now you must prove yours. I've already told you my name. What are you called?"

The alien stared at her for a long moment, trying to

decide what to do. Finally, realizing that he had no alternative but to trust her, he said "Grgat Dranna Rzinika."

"All right, Grgat Dranna Rzinika, would you care to tell me why you hid aboard my ship?"

"I was running away."

"From whom?"

"From the gods." The computer translated the words in a near monotone, but it didn't take a degree in alienology for Dev to detect the bitterness and disgust in the creature's voice.

"Why?" When the native hesitated a moment, Dev added, "Remember, they can't hear you while you're in this ship. You can speak freely."

"I hate them!" Grgat exploded suddenly. "They are cruel and unfeeling. I would rather give my support to the demons of the outer skies than live any longer under the domination of these gods."

"Am I a demon, then?"

Grgat looked her over carefully. "No, you seem to be a mortal being like me, although you do have mystical powers. But you come from the realm the demons hold, and . . . and I was hoping you would take me back there with you."

Dev moved away from the door over to the cot where her captive sat. She sat down at the opposite edge, careful not to make any sudden motions that could be interpreted as threatening. "I'm not trying to be argumentative," she said, "but I have to know your motives. *Why* do you hate the gods? *Why* are you risking your life to escape from them?"

The other's clawlike hands twitched nervously. "Because they killed my wife Sennet. They killed her without mercy for merely following her natural instincts. They . . ."

Dev interrupted his incipient diatribe. "Did Sennet speak out against them?"

"No, that was the irony. She was a loyal and true believer. She was always chiding me to be more worshipful."

"Then why did they kill her?"

"Because she got pregnant. Our village was already up to its allotted quota, and even after some people died—including our only daughter—they refused permission to increase. It should have been our turn next, but when Sennet became pregnant the gods sent one of their messengers to take the child from her belly. In front of the whole village she begged and pleaded with the angel not to take our baby. She was most respectful as she begged, but even so—just to show the futility of arguing with the gods—they killed her. Then, because our village was now well below quota, they gave the allotment to the next couple on the list."

By the time he was finished speaking, Grgat was looking down at his feet, avoiding Dev's eyes completely. "I cannot worship beings who would do such a cruel thing to a follower as loyal as Sennet. I don't care if they are gods, or if they can kill me with but a single thought—I cannot worship them."

"No," Dev said softly—so softly that her computer almost failed to pick it up and translate it. "No, I wouldn't expect you to." All her instincts cried out for her to put a comforting arm around Grgat's shoulders—but she was afraid the alien might misinterpret the gesture. So instead her hands remained sedately in her lap.

Grgat continued as though he hadn't heard her. "That's why, when your ship arrived a few days later, I resolved to hide aboard it and travel up into the realm of the demons. Surely they couldn't be any worse than the gods I've had to endure. When a shipment of ore was loaded aboard your ship this afternoon, I hid down inside it and was brought in here. That's where I've been until you found me. I meant you no harm, I swear it."

"I believe you," Dev said. Then, as an afterthought, she added, "You must be awfully hungry, though, if you've been in here all day without food."

"I am. But I expect to suffer."

"Nonsense. Even the worst prisoners are entitled to eat—and whatever your status is, you're above that. Your body chemistry isn't too different from ours—I think we can find you something nourishing, if not quite what you're used to."

Dev got up, went over to the door, and opened it. "Bakori," she called, sticking her head outside.

In a moment she could see the form of the astrogator appear below. "Yes, Captain?"

"Our prisoner hasn't eaten for a while. Go to the galley and fix him something to tide him over until we can decide what to do with him."

"Yes, ma'am."

As the astrogator moved to comply with her order, Roscil Larramac appeared below. "Has he started to talk, then?"

"Well enough," Dev replied. "He's in a lot of trouble outside."

"He's in trouble here, too. I want to talk to him. Be right up." Larramac started up the ladder to her level.

Dev warned Grgat that the ship's owner was going to be coming in, but that Larramac meant no harm and only wanted to talk. The native looked a bit more nervous—he had only just gotten used to the idea of talking to Dev—but he was obviously in no position to object.

When Larramac entered, Dev quickly filled him in on what Grgat had told her thus far. After she had finished, Larramac was silent for a moment, running one hand thoughtfully through his goatee. Finally he said, "If we take him on, we may run into trouble from these local deities, whoever they are. Is it worth it, Dev?"

"I don't have enough information yet. But I intend to." Turning to Grgat, she said, "We'll have to know a little more before we can help you. Tell us absolutely everything you know about the gods."

4

> "Ride with the moment. Even if it's unpleasant, there'll
> always be another along shortly."
> —Anthropos, *The Sane Mind*

Before the Beginning [Grgat explained] there was nothing but the Primal Mist permeating the Universe. It
was uniform and without shape. Then, over a period of
ages, it began to coalesce into distinct entities, which
eventually became the gods and the demons. At first,
these two races coexisted in peaceful harmony. Together, they created the stars and the worlds out of
remnants of Primal Mist, and they imposed order on a
chaotic cosmos.

But, after many eons, the two races had a falling out.
The gods wanted to create mortal creatures with whom
they could share the wonders of the Universe; the
demons selfishly sought to prevent other life and to
hoard their secrets for themselves. The two philoso-
phies proved incompatible, and a war was the natural
consequence.

The heavens themselves erupted in fire as the two
species of deities vied for supremacy. Stars exploded,
planets were devastated in the battles that ensued.
Finally, to prevent further destruction, the gods asked
for and received a truce. The planet Dascham was
created as a place where the gods could experiment
with life to their souls' content, while the demons
agreed to roam about the heavens and not interfere
with matters on Dascham.

The gods built a mountain called Orrork, where they
made their home, and where they continue to dwell
even to this day. Once they settled in, they made the
members of the Daschamese race in their own image to

44

assist them in their study of the mysteries of the Universe.

At first, the gods and the mortals mingled as equals. But then, some evil Daschamese began to grow conceited, and to think they were better than the gods. They started a revolt, which the gods, with their far superior powers, were able to quell quickly—the Time of the Burning. But the gods knew that their creations, the Daschamese, were flawed—their head-strong conceits would always lead them to be challenging their creators. Some of the gods thought to destroy all the Daschamese and begin their experiments with life afresh, but others of their colleagues demurred. Eventually it was decided that the Daschamese should be kept, but as slaves, fit only for worship of the gods and for menial labor in serving them. The gods would keep a constant watch on their disobedient servants, ever alert for further signs of rebellion. In addition, the gods created the angels to remind the Daschamese of their debased status and to reprimand and punish all who would transgress against the will of the gods.

A strict code of regulations was established. No Daschamese would say or do anything to indicate hostility toward the gods. Sacrifices of food would be gathered at intervals from each village and taken by the angels to the mountain Orrork. The Daschamese, in addition to raising food for themselves, had to work at various tasks for the gods—mining specified minerals and rocks, which were put in large bins and collected by the angels.

Freedoms were limited in numerous ways. Population control was strictly enforced. No more than sixteen Daschamese were ever allowed to assemble in any one place at the same time. The Daschamese had no written language, and the gods listened in on every conversation that was spoken, no matter how quietly whispered. Retribution (as Dev had seen earlier) was swift and definite for any who chose to disobey the will of the gods.

The gods were invincible, and they ruled Dascham with a will of iron.

Dev and her boss listened quietly as Grgat explained the theology of Dascham. When the native was finished, a silence fell over the cabin. Finally Larramac reached over and switched off the translator on Dev's headset so Grgat would not know what they were saying. "What do you think?" he asked.

"It makes for a nice story."

"But do you believe it?" Larramac eyed her narrowly.

"I assume from your odd glance that Dunnis filled you in on my theories about the gods. No, I don't believe it literally. It bears much in common with creation myths of primitive peoples all over the Galaxy. I do think, though, that there's more truth in this one than there is in most of them. And I do believe in the powers of the gods; I saw them demonstrated only too well this evening."

Larramac was silent for a moment, then reached for Dev's headset. Dev handed it to him and he switched on the translator once again. "Tell me, Grgat, what exactly do you expect of us?"

"I would like you to take me away from Dascham, into the sky, into the realm of the demons."

"But you just told us the demons are opposed to life. Why should you want to go there?"

The native hesitated, then finally decided to trust the human. "I ... I wanted to ask their help in destroying the gods. Only when the gods are defeated can Dascham be truly free."

"Would the demons even listen to you? How could you expect to gain their sympathy when they're so opposed to life?"

"The gods claim to be good, yet I've seen them do some things that even they say are bad. They claim to be wise, yet sometimes they act foolishly. I'm learning very quickly not to believe everything the gods have told me."

"The onset of wisdom," Dev muttered—but very quietly, so that the translator would not pick it up.

Grgat went on, oblivious to her remark. "The gods say that the demons would not tolerate life—yet you come from the heavens and you are tolerated, though you are neither demons nor gods. The gods claim to know everything on Daschaïn, yet they obviously don't know what we are saying now or they would have struck us down long before this."

"How do you propose to find the demons?" Dev asked.

"I don't know," the native admitted. "Have you ever met any?"

"I've met a number of beings who could fit the term, but they're probably not the ones you have in mind."

"Would you perhaps help me look for them? You could be paid well."

At the mention of payment, Larramac sat up a bit straighter. He focused his attention much more keenly on Grgat's ursine form as he said, "Pay? How? I didn't know you Daschamese had anything to pay with. You don't look particularly wealthy."

"It would have to be after the gods were destroyed, of course. If we were no longer having to serve them, we could labor to pay off our debt to others. There are minerals that the gods consider valuable, and some for which you also wish to trade. We could supply much more of that in exchange for our freedom."

At this moment the ship's astrogator, Lian Bakori, entered with a tray of food for the prisoner. From the eager look on Grgat's face as he eyed the food, Dev judged it would be best to break off the interrogation for now. They were all tired and in need of rest. So, after Bakori set the tray down, she left the cabin, shooing the owner and the astrogator out ahead of her.

Outside once more, Dunnis approached her. "Look what I found, Captain."

The tiny piece of metal he held in his outstretched hand was less than two centimeters long; though it had a small set of legs for mobility, it was obviously artificial.

"Where'd you find that?" she asked.

"In the hold, while we were cleaning up. You were right, I think it's one of the bugs those gods use."

Dev was feeling too tired to derive any pleasure from having her assumptions proved correct. She merely

47

took a deep breath and said, "Can you discover what frequency it's broadcasting on?"

"It may take a little while, but . . . yeah, I can."

"Good. Do so immediately. Then I'll want you to build a jamming device so that I can turn off the meteoroid deflectors. We're eating into the ship's power."

"Yes, Captain. It may take a while."

"Take all the time you need, up to 0730 this morning. Then it better be ready."

"But, Captain, I haven't had any sleep, and the tests . . ."

"If you hadn't been out carousing with Zhurat, none of this would be necessary. And the tests are relatively straightforward—I do have some knowledge of engineering. I could do the tests and build the jammer myself in fifteen hours; I expect you, with your special expertise in the subject, to do it in half the time."

Dunnis opened his mouth to protest further, but Dev cut him off. "Every minute you stand here arguing with me gives you one less minute in which to work. I'd suggest you get started now."

The engineer shrugged his massive shoulders and lumbered off to comply with her orders, leaving her alone with Larramac and Bakori. "I'll be in my cabin if I'm needed," she told the two men. "I have this very strong suspicion that tonight's activities are only a prelude to something far worse, and I'd like to get at least a few hours' rest before having to deal with it."

Bakori accepted her announcement with the same stony silence he used for all occasions. The astrogator was an orthodox Neo-Buddhist and, as such, accepted the entire Universe exactly as it happened. Dev could not recall ever meeting a more passive man . . . but he performed his job reasonably well and he gave her no trouble, so she had no complaints.

Roscil Larramac, though, was another matter. He was still brooding over what Grgat had said—and the abstracted look on his face boded little good. *I wish I knew what was going on inside that overeager brain of his,* Dev thought. *But whatever it is, I know I'm not going to like it.*

* * *

Despite her announced intention of getting some sleep, she found it a scarce commodity tonight. She lay atop the covers on her fold-down cot, her eyes roaming restlessly around the room. There was a toilet and washbasin crammed together in one corner and a set of built-in drawers to hold most of her personal belongings. The bare metal walls had few things to catch her attention: loops for stringing the zero-gee hammock that was currently folded away in a drawer; a chronometer; a picture of her parents and one of the dormitory where she'd spent her first seven years; a few shots of the planets she'd visited; and a sampler with her favorite quotation from Anthropos, "Don't pray for miracles—create them!"

She wondered idly whether she'd be up to the task this time. Within the space of several hours her problems had undergone a logarithmic increase, and would not let her mind rest easily.

She picked up a microspool idly and scanned through it; but even reading, her favorite pastime, held little interest after tonight's activities. Disturbed that she could not lose herself so easily, she set the spool viewer down on the floor beside her.

All problems have solutions, she reminded herself. *It merely requires setting the mind in order.* Determined to do so, she separated her worries into their discrete components and examined them individually.

First, the gods. Her speech to the angel seemed to have appeased their anger over Zhurat's outburst, but they would still be on their guard against the humans. The *Foxfire* crew was a potentially disruptive influence in a world they strove to keep static—and her action of turning on the deflector screens would only increase their suspicions. The humans would be under close scrutiny from this point on; all their outward appearances would have to be letter perfect, or they would draw more of the gods' wrath.

Second, the stowaway. The gods might not yet know he was missing, but once they learned they could easily jump to the correct conclusion that he was hiding in the human ship. How would they react? Would they demand that the humans deliver him up to their justice? If they did, should she do so? The ethics of the situation were incredibly tangled, and her response could affect human-Daschamese trading relations for centuries.

Third, the guns. Larramac had deliberately kept them secret from her, just as he had kept their itinerary secret. "I'll tell you where we're going when you have to go there," he'd said, and all her attempts to drag further information from him had been futile. She knew he hadn't been attempting to sell the guns here; the gods would never have tolerated that. But the weapons worried her all the same. Gunrunning was not illegal; nothing was in space, where human laws could not reach. But it would add complications to this trading mission that she would have to plan for.

Besides, she considered dealing in armaments immoral. An Eoan didn't really care whether other people chose to blast themselves out of existence—but it was considered bad form to help them along the way.

Having thus enumerated the problems she would have to deal with, she then began a list of the resources at her disposal.

First, the crew. Everyone aboard was some sort of misfit. Roscil Larramac, she had learned, was pushy, ambitious, overreaching, and greedy in addition to being superstitious, condescending, brash, occasionally charming, sometimes generous, and extremely intelligent. Zhurat had been marginally competent and professionally quarrelsome; well, he was no longer a factor. Lian Bakori would do as he was told and absolutely nothing more; he was a good astrogator, but his Neo-Buddhist leanings meant he practiced the principle of Minimal Involvement. Gros Dunnis was competent and affable, but lazy in the extreme; Dev had found it necessary to build a fire under him any time something needed doing. There were twenty robots, heavy-duty machines with great strength and minds slightly higher than moron level. And, to round out the complement, she included herself: an Eoan captain, quite competent but a harsh disciplinarian, and endowed with all the legendary qualities of arrogance and superior self-righteousness for which Eoàns were notorious. It was not the way she liked to think of herself, but the situation called for objectivity.

Second, the ship. *Foxfire* was a small freighter, with a cargo hold heavy with miscellaneous merchandise. The ship itself was unarmed, but carried with it a weapon of enormous power—its gravitic drive's back-wash. The electromagnetic energies released in the wake of a starship as it took off or landed were devasta-ting. Living tissue fried almost instantly within that field; electronic equipment burned out; metals melted. One of the first safety lessons drilled into anyone who worked in or around starships was that the backwash was instant death and destruction. It could—and had, on occasion— been used as an instrument of war.

Third, the stowaway. Although he wouldn't be able to function aboard the ship, he'd be a mine of informa-tion about the planet Dascham. Already he'd furnished some invaluable clues about the history and social organization of this world; should they encounter fur-ther trouble with the gods, he might provide other leads as well. Assuming, of course, that she didn't turn him over to the gods upon demand.

Fourth, the guns. As with Grgat, these were a re-source as well as a potential problem. She hated the thought of using violence . . . but she hated even worse the thought of anyone else using violence on her. If the gods decided to get nasty, Dev had the wherewithal to be equally nasty in return. And she would not hesitate to use it.

Having sorted things out, her mind felt more re-laxed. There was nothing she could do at present about the problems that were still waiting to surface. But she knew where to expect them and what she could use to combat them, which was the maximum preparation possible under the circumstances. She concentrated once more on going to sleep.

Her eyes had barely closed, though, when there was a gentle knocking at her door. Struggling out of her sleepy fog, she glanced at the chronometer set in the wall. It was 0600, far too early for Dunnis to have finished his task. "Who's there?" she asked, knowing there could be only one answer.

"It's Roscil." She'd guessed correctly. "May I come in and talk with you privately?"

"Just a minute." She swung off her cot and looked at herself in the mirror above the washbasin. Her thin face looked even more haggard and worried than usual, making her seem older than she really was. *I really ought to smile more; it would do wonders for my appearance,* she thought as she ran a comb quickly through her tangled hair. *Though Space only knows what there is to smile about these days.*

The spacer uniform she was wearing was disheveled after the day's hectic activities, so she reached into her drawer for a fresh one. As were all its cousins, this uniform was a one-piece, loose-fitting jumpsuit that covered the entire body from neck down. It included gloves and boots, and sealed with a single seam down the front. Elastic bands at wrists, waist, and ankles prevented unmanageable ballooning in freefall, and the entire ensemble could be converted into a spacesuit with the simple addition of helmet and air tanks. A row of gauges, including a watch, circled her waist as a belt.

The spacer uniforms were universal wear in human spaceships, but there was still room for individual embellishments. Each person had his own distinctive color code and design to set himself apart from everyone else. Dev's uniform was mostly brown, with a wide stripe of light green running from right shoulder to left hip down the front and up again across the back. Over her left breast she displayed her emblem of captaincy, and with it the logo of Elliptic Enterprises.

Thus attired, she was once again presentable to entertain company. "All right, come in."

Larramac entered. From the slightly bloodshot appearance of his eyes and the small bags under them, Dev guessed that he hadn't slept much this night, either. "I've been thinking," he began, "about what that native said."

Dev sat silently watching him. She was content, at this point, to let him do all the talking.

"We obviously can't take him to the demons, because we don't know where they are ourselves. The way I interpret his myth is that there was a space war hundreds, maybe thousands, of years ago. A band of the losers landed here, and used their superior technology to enslave the natives. For all we know, the 'demons'—who are merely the winning side in the war—may have become extinct long before Man ever left Earth. Does all this sound right to you?"

Dev nodded sleepily, wondering when he would stop expounding on the obvious.

"So, the demons won't be able to help our friend. But maybe we could."

Dev chose to speak now. "How?"

"By getting rid of the gods, as he asked. We know they're not supernatural beings; all their effects, as you yourself pointed out, are things that we could duplicate."

"Yes, but they're operating on a scale we couldn't begin to equal. Their electronic surveillance covers everything that happens all over the surface of Dascham. Think of what their computer facilities alone must be like if they can correlate all that data instantaneously— and they can, because I've seen the results."

Larramac dismissed that with a wave of his hand. "I don't care what their computers are like. Computers aren't weapons."

"Those angels are. They've got self-contained gravitic engines that could backwash us at any time. They're also pretty accurate with a lightning bolt."

"A ship in the air could outmaneuver them so that we wouldn't have to worry about their backwash. And those lightning bolts wouldn't work much damage on the ship."

"They may have bigger weapons stashed away for an emergency."

"You're certainly being very negative this morning," Larramac grumbled.

"As captain, it's my duty to place the safety of the ship at the highest priority. If I were any less cautious, I'd suggest you fire me because I wouldn't be worth my pay."

Larramac grinned. "Okay. But remember, these are the losers in a war. They came here in defeat. Any large weapons they had would probably no longer function."

"They've had plenty of time to rebuild—and the Daschamese provide them with plenty of raw materials and labor."

Larramac took a deep breath and let it out again. "Nevertheless, I'm prepared to take the risk."

Dev asked her second big question of the morning. "Why?"

Her boss blinked and looked at her. "You heard him. He said they'd pay nicely if we got rid of the gods. There's all that duty the natives currently give to them that we could be getting instead."

"Grgat is hardly the planetary leader. He's not in a negotiating position. He can't make an offer on behalf of his entire planet."

Larramac was becoming increasingly impatient. His tone of voice was snappish as he replied, "I've learned that when one man says something, a million more are thinking it. All these people are waiting for is their freedom. They'll be so happy to get it that they'll give their liberators anything they've got."

"Are you suggesting, then, that we fly back and recruit an assault squad to kill off these gods?"

"No I'm not. Surprise is the most important asset we have. Even now the gods might suspect us of ulterior motives; giving them another couple of months to prepare for a fight would only decrease our chances of success."

And bringing more people in on the job would also

54

decrease your share of the spoils, Dev thought cynically. *See how well I'm getting to know you, Roscil?*

"Then the only alternative," she said aloud, "is that we make our attack with the personnel and equipment we have available now."

"Exactly. What's your opinion?"

"How nice of you to finally ask. My opinion is that this idea is stupid, ill-conceived, reckless, and, in general, utterly without merit. I think we should conclude our trading today as scheduled and depart at once for our next destination—wherever that is—leaving behind us all thoughts of deicide."

Her boss was taken aback by the vehemence of her words. "At least listen to my plan before calling it names. According to Grgat, all the gods live in one place, this mountain they call Orrork. We conclude our trading tomorrow as we said we'd do and take off—but instead of leaving, we orbit around and then come down again on their mountain. They'd never be able to survive our backwash if we landed right on top of them; there'd be almost no risk at all."

"Is that your plan?"

"In essence, yes."

"Good. Now that I've listened to it, I *still* think it's stupid, ill-conceived, and reckless."

Larramac set his jaw firmly. "I'm paying you to do what I order, Dev."

"Wrong. You're paying me to captain your ship and complete the trading mission your company has established. My duties do not include leading a suicidal attack on the local establishment. I'm a pilot, not a mercenary."

"I could fire you, you know."

Dev looked mildly amused. "Do you like Dascham well enough to settle here, then? Without me, you'll never get the ship off the ground."

"Oh yes I will. You may not know it, but I pilot my own airplane back on New Crete. I can take the controls here and make the attack myself if I choose."

The expression of amusement vanished from Dev's

face. "The controls of a starship are at least a dozen times more complex than those of an airplane. You'd kill us all trying a stunt like that."

"We're going to attack that citadel, Dev. If you're not at the controls, I will be. Take your choice."

Dev ran quickly through her list of options. She could refuse and risk having the ship crash due to Larramac's inexperience. She knew entirely too well the enormous amount of patience and sensitivity required to handle the controls of a ship like *Foxfire;* and patience and sensitivity were not two of her boss's more outstanding assets. They would all be doomed if Larramac were allowed behind the control console.

She considered the possibility of sabotaging the ship so that he couldn't fly it, but rejected that idea as well. If she performed any major sabotage, she wouldn't be able to fly the ship either, and they would all be stranded here indefinitely. If the sabotage were less severe, Dunnis—who would certainly follow his boss's instructions over hers—would be able to fix it or compensate for it.

As Larramac said, it was either him or her. The raid on the gods might have only one chance of success in a million, but those odds were still better with her in command than with him at the helm.

She sighed loudly. "You win, Roscil, but I warn you: I'll be filing a complaint with the Starship Pilots' Guild the instant we get back to civilization—if we ever do."

"We will, don't worry. We'll go through the rest of today as though nothing out of the ordinary is happening, then make our plans tonight." He turned and left her cabin.

Dev sat on the edge of her bunk, collecting her thoughts. It was an unfortunate fact of the Universe that insanity frequently accompanied the power to put one's neuroses into action despite all sane advice to the contrary. Short of outright mutiny, there was no way she could alter her employer's plans; she would have to, instead, see that they were carried out in the best and safest manner possible.

My problem, she thought, *is that I listed Roscil as one of my resources instead of one of my potential trouble spots. As the old saying goes, if you're not part of the solution, you're part of the problem.*

Roscil Larramac, she decided, was definitely part of the problem.

5

"Where is security to be found? In a universe of constant surprises and disappointments, it's foolish to look for external sources . . . The sane person is, first and foremost, secure within himself."

—Anthropos, *The Sane Mind*

There was no point to going back to sleep; she would have to get up soon anyway to begin the day's activities. Dev freshened up, washed her face, and managed to squeeze in a chapter from a recent popularized microspool on comparative interplanetary ichthyology before it was time for her to emerge from her cabin and officially start the day.

She wandered into *Foxfire*'s tiny galley and discovered that breakfast had not been made. She had instituted a schedule for cooking at the very beginning of this voyage, in which even she and Larramac took turns preparing meals. But breakfast today had been Dunnis's responsibility, and he was busy working on the jammer she'd requested. In all the confusion of last night, she had forgotten to rearrange the assignment. *Whenever anything's out of place on a ship,* she reminded herself, *it's always the captain's ultimate responsibility to see it's put right again.*

With a tired sigh she began fixing a quick, easy meal for the entire crew. It would not be gourmet quality, but it would do. *I love to eat good food,* she thought, *but I've never gotten the knack of cooking it right.* And she also made a note to mention to everyone else that Zhurat's death caused the chores rotation to move up one.

The rest of *Foxfire*'s complement, with the exception of Grgat, who was still under guard, began assembling just as she finished. Dunnis was quite late, not appearing until close to 0800, but he had the jammer completed and working. It would, he assured Dev, provide sufficient interference to deaden all bugs within a radius of forty meters or so—meaning the entire ship would be safe ground for conversations. Dev nodded and made no mention that he was over her deadline; she was sure he'd done his job well.

By the time breakfast was finished and she was able to go outside with Larramac, the natives had already arrived. They circled the ship, about forty of them, with their crude wagons laden to overflowing with ore. Dascham, it had been found, had some rich deposits of monazite, samarskite, thortveitite, and other rare-earth minerals, and of such gem minerals as turquoise, alexandrite and tourmaline; it was for these that parties of humans came to the planet and traded. The gods did not object to the Daschamese receiving knives and other manufactured utensils that were infinitely better made than their own crude implements. Only the fact that the payment to the Daschamese was so cheap made Dascham a worth-while trading stop for Larramac's company.

With Zhurat dead, Dev knew it was incumbent on her to supervise the robots in their task of transferring the minerals from the natives' carts to the waiting bins aboard ship. She ordered all twenty on the job, leaving none to guard their stowaway.

"Do you think that's wise?" Larramac asked her.

"How could it hurt? Grgat can't leave the ship or the gods will kill him. He hasn't the training to steal the ship, and I've told him not to touch anything if he wants to reach the demons, so I don't think he'll do any damage. It'll be hard enough as it is for me to take over Zhurat's job; I don't need to be shorthanded as well."

While Larramac inspected the merchandise he was buying and argued with the Daschamese leaders about the quality of the ore and the rates of exchange, Dev got her score of robots lined up and issued their initial instructions. The bargaining didn't take as long as she would have thought; the Daschamese were exceptionally docile, and took pretty much what the humans offered. The gods had evidently bred most of the aggressiveness out of them.

The haggling completed, she set about her task of supervising the robots. She had never done this particular job before, although she had studied others doing it. She found it was far more difficult to do than to watch. It was as though the robots looked for ambiguities and errors in every order she gave and followed through with erroneous glee. Her eyes had to be everywhere, and she found herself dashing all over the work area to tell some robot that no, she hadn't meant he should load the entire wagon into the ship, just its contents; or that the transfer container had sprung a leak and he should get a new one; or that he should go around a *daryek* rather than through it.

No wonder Zhurat was always so foul-tempered, she thought. *If it was my job to nursemaid these twenty high-grade morons all the time, I'd turn pretty sour myself.*

Toward afternoon, the workload began to slacken. Most of the carts had been off-loaded and Larramac was busy parceling out the agreed-upon payments. Dev felt dead on her feet after the excitement of the previous night, the lack of sleep, the chasing after the robots, and the prospect of her boss's upcoming military adventure. She would have liked nothing better than to go to her cabin and collapse for at least several hours—but there was something she knew she had to check first.

She began a gentle meandering away from the ship. Their backwash had burned a bare area in this field for thirty meters around their touchdown point, but beyond that the ground was covered with wildflowers. *All the rain here must be great for them,* she thought, for they existed in profusion—a gay mixture of yellows, greens, and blues, with hints of a few other colors scattered about for variety. Most of the plants were tall enough to reach halfway up her calf, and a few of the more venturesome species came as high as her waist. They all waved slightly in the late afternoon breeze that heralded the approach of another nocturnal rainstorm.

She was not looking for flowers, though, but for objects that were far smaller and much less conspicuous. Having seen one of the gods' bugs last night, she knew what they looked like—though finding them in this profusion of vegetation was another matter.

By craning her head at odd angles, she managed to catch the reflection of sunlight off the bugs' polished metal surfaces—they were the only metal around. After about an hour of wandering about, she had spotted enough of them to make a rough estimate of their distribution pattern. They were so numerous that no bug was more than five meters away from any other and in some places—along the side of the road, for example—they were even denser than that.

The enormity of the gods' operation was frightening. Even if the bugs were only distributed near inhabited areas and not uniformly over all of Dascham's land surface, there would have to be billions upon billions of the little mechanisms happily broadcasting away to their headquarters—and most of the time they would have nothing to report. Manufacturing them would have to be a full-time process, too; Dev doubted the lifetime of the components would exceed two years. The process of removing and reseeding all those billions of microphones every couple of years would be phenomenal.

Added to that would be the immense complexity of assimilating all the data once it was gathered. It could only be done by computer, she knew. The image came to her of kilomater after kilometer of compter banks, doing nothing but listening to the sounds broadcast by the bugs, checking them for possible significance. If the sounds should be interpreted as Daschamese conversation, it would be further correlated for meaning and possible heretical content. Assuming one of the natives was saying something naughty, the computers would then have to find the miscreant and punish him. That could be done, she supposed, by comparing the input from all the neighboring bugs and triangulating the position. Using voiceprint identification, it could even be possible to learn which particular Daschamese was speaking out of line; everything about his past life could be recalled instantly from the memory banks, and a judgment made about what particular punishment would fit this crime. Then one of the angels—which were probably stationed in local hiding places near the settlements—would be dispatched to deal with the problem.

That, at least, would be the way Dev would set it up if she were running such an operation. Given the resources of an entire planet, it would not be beyond the bounds of reason.

And this was the operation Larramac thought he could demolish with but a single cargo ship? If she weren't in such an unenviable position, she would have considered it laughable. But ridiculous or not, she had little choice in the matter—she would have to make it work. *Don't pray for miracles—create them!*

As she started back toward *Foxfire* she could hear a slight whirring noise in the air above her. Looking up into the graying sky, she caught sight of one of the angels descending. She stopped where she was, not wanting inadvertently to wander directly under it and be killed by the backwash of its gravitic drive.

As was the case the night before, the angel stopped its descent while it was still a good five meters above the ground and ten meters in front of her. Dev was half expecting it to run through the entire preliminary ritual of last night, but instead it addressed her directly. "Captain Korrell." It spoke in Galingua, a chilling thought. Its computers must have analyzed the human language from past trading missions.

"I hear the voice of the gods, and I obey," Dev replied humbly.

"The gods seek to know the whereabouts of the being named Grgat Dranna Rzinika."

Dev feigned innocence. " 'Seek to know'? I thought the gods knew everything."

If the angel detected her sarcasm, it failed to react to it. "We know now that Grgat Dranna Rzinika could only have hidden inside your vessel late yesterday afternoon."

Dev saw no advantage to denying it. "That is true."

"He has violated our laws and blasphemed against the gods. We demand that you release him to our custody so that he may be punished accordingly."

This is it, she thought. *Confrontation number one.* She had wondered earlier whether she should give Grgat over to the gods to appease them, or whether she should stick to her moral principles and give him the sanctuary he requested. But now a new factor had been added. If they did indeed make this attack on the gods' citadel, they would need Grgat's knowledge of Daschamese lore. The decision had been made for her. "I can't do that," she said evenly.

The angel's eyes glowed a slightly brighter red. "Do you defy the gods?"

"Not at all. It's just that your demand is physically impossible. When Grgat hid away aboard our ship without permission, he was in violation of our own laws. As soon as we found him, he was summarily executed."

That answer made the angel pause for a full second before continuing. "In that case, produce the body for our inspection."

"Again, I regret that's impossible. In accordance with out own customs, his body was immediately fed into our matter converter and recycled into more useful form."

"You must offer us some proof of your words."

"How can I, when none exists? Had I known of the gods' interest in this matter I would of course have saved the body for your inspection. But I repeat, I was only acting in accordance with the customs of my own people. If the gods feel I am lying, they may take appropriate measures—but I swear on the gods' own names that I am telling only the truth."

Dev was taking a calculated risk here, and she knew it. There was nothing to stop the gods from tossing a lightning bolt at her on general principles if they felt like it. Trade with the humans was not so vital to their interests that they would regret losing it by taking a face-saving action. On the other hand, by showing herself willing to die to prove her point, she gave the gods nothing to *gain* by killing her, either. Killing Zhurat had enhanced their prestige and respect; Dev's death would net them nothing of the sort.

I hope they think along the same lines, she thought as she stood rigidly below the angel, waiting for its decision. She knew, also, that the gods were aware the humans were jamming the bugs from inside the ship; but they would never admit that publicly.

The seconds dragged on interminably, and at last the angel spoke. "The gods decree that no punishment will be required, and that you acted entirely within your own customs. But now, since your business on Dascham is at an end, we demand that you and your ship depart quickly."

"I agree," Dev said, an unshown wave of relief washing through her body. "It will yet take us several hours of preparation before our vessel is ready to go, but I promise we will have lifted off before midnight, local time." That was not strictly true—they could have been ready within an hour or two if necessary. But she wanted to allow herself some leeway.

The angel did not answer. It merely waved the flaming sword it carried in a gesture of farewell and lifted once more into the sky. Dev stood where she was until its shape was lost in the general grayness of the clouds, then continued her walk back to *Foxfire.*

Larramac was waiting for her. He had seen and, apparently, heard most or all of the exchange. He started to say something, but Dev quickly put a finger to her lips, calling for silence. She gestured her head toward the ship, indicating that they should wait until they were safely inside and within the jamming field before they spoke about it.

As the last of the Daschamese were paid off, the carts were driven away, including the one that *Foxfire*'s crew had used temporarily. Dev herded the robots back into the ship, then she and her boss clambered into the airlock, shutting the outer hatch behind them.

"You really had me worried there," Larramac finally said. "You were taking quite a risk."

"I had me worried, too. And the risk I was taking is a

Sunday stroll compared to what you have in mind. Have you any idea what we're up against?"

"I have a feeling you're going to tell me."

And for once, Larramac was right. His captain spent several minutes explaining the distribution of the bugs and the computerized information analysis system that would logically have to accompany it. Repeatedly she emphasized the scale on which the gods worked. But Larramac remained unswayed in his intentions.

"I'm not questioning the efficiency of their intelligence network. But computers are not offensive weapons. All their armament, all their vast resources, have been directed against primitive creatures who are barely more than savages. They couldn't withstand an attack by their technological equals because they haven't needed to for hundreds, maybe thousands, of years. They've gone soft.

"Just look at what you, by yourself, were able to accomplish. Standing out there alone in that field, without even reaching for your pistol, you faced down an angel, the very symbol of the gods' authority. You told it a blatant lie and dared it to do anything—and it backed down. Do you know why?"

"No, why?"

"Because the gods don't know our capabilities. We look like a harmless trading ship, but they can't be positive and they dared not take the chance. They're afraid of us."

"I think 'cautious' would be a better adjective than 'afraid,' " she said as she opened the inner door of the airlock and stepped into the familiar corridor of the ship.

Bakori had prepared the dinner, and Dev invited Grgat to eat with them in the mess hall. There would have to be a war council now, while they were all together, and Grgat would play a central role in their eventual decisions.

At Dev's insistence, she was the one who told the others what they were going to be doing; no matter what her personal feelings, it was the captain's responsibility to give the orders to the crew. Bakori accepted the news passively, as though she'd told him it would rain tonight. Dunnis was much more dubious about the venture, but she had him sufficiently cowed by this time that he would say nothing to contradict her directly.

Then she turned on her translator and informed Grgat that they would not take him to the demons, but instead would destroy the gods themselves. The Daschamese was delighted.

"We will need some further information from you," Dev continued. "Are you sure that all the gods live together in one place?"

"Yes. They have no other home than Orrork."

"Good. Then it should all be decided by one action. Where is this Mount Orrork?"

"It is over in that direction, so I'm told." Grgat waved a paw in the general vicinity of the northeast.

"How far from here?"

"I do not know."

"I love the specific directions," Dunnis muttered. "There's probably only fifty thousand mountains out that way."

Dev turned off her headset and faced the big engineer. "I will not tolerate negative thinking. If this operation succeeds, it will be because each one of us does his best to make it work. I won't accept less than total co-operation, is that clear?"

Dunnis nodded glumly.

Larramac, meanwhile, had brought out the humans' crude maps of Dascham, as drawn by previous traders. While these maps had been drafted by amateurs, they were intended for use by ships' pilots and contained sufficient detail to make an educated guess.

"Here's where we are now," Larramac said to Grgat, pointing to a spot on the map. "Where is Orrork in relation to this?"

The native blinked uncomprehendingly at the charts. "We are not there, we're here," and he pointed straight downward. "Orrork is over there." And again he pointed to the northeast.

Larramac shook his head. "No, this spot on the map

represents our position. This direction"—he indicated "north" on the map—"means that way." He pointed north in real life.

Grgat only looked more confused. "How can this way be that way? They are two different things."

Dev sat by, mildly amused by the encounter, but finally she decided to end the debate. "You're wasting your time, Roscil. The Daschamese have no written language, and they seem to have little or no concept of representational symbols. Where you point on a map is only a spot on a piece of paper to him; he can't translate it into physical reality. It would probably take a year or better to train him to think symbolically, and we haven't got the time."

The boss snorted. "Then how do *you* suggest we find where Orrork is?"

"We look for the biggest source of radio emission on the planet. With the primitive level of technology here, we know the natives aren't broadcasting. The bugs are, but their signals will be coming from all over, more or less uniformly, like background noise. If the gods control this planet from one central spot, then they will be constantly having to broadcast their orders and information to be angels and any substations.

"As was the case with the bugs, we don't know what frequency they're broadcasting on, but that's just a technical detail. What I'd suggest is that we go up into orbit and examine the mountain ranges to the northeast of this village to see which one is broadcasting. If that doesn't work, we'll have to think of some other method of finding our target." *Or abandon the search entirely*, Dev hoped. Sometimes she wished she weren't so competent; if Larramac had not trusted in her abilities, he would never have suggested the raid. And if she were not so dedicated, she would have hidden her ideas on how to locate Orrork.

Larramac was nodding slowly as she spoke. "Yes, that sounds good."

"What do you propose after we've found the place?"

"We come down on it tail first, wiping out everything immediately below us with our backwash."

67

Dev grimaced despite herself. "That's awfully simplistic."

"The best tactics always are."

So are the worst, Dev thought, but refrained from voicing her doubts in front of the rest of the crew.

6

"By the eighteenth century, scientists knew that every action has an equal and opposite reaction. Awareness of that fact has put the physical sciences centuries ahead of the social sciences."

—Anthropos, *Sanity and Society*

After the conference broke up, it took another two hours before the ship was ready for lift-off. The procedure itself was not nearly that involved but, again, they were shorthanded. It was normally Zhurat's duty to check out the robots and the cargo area, making sure that everything was safely stowed away in its place. Having something even slightly out of alignment could be disastrous when the internal acceleration reached two g's; a box even slightly off-center could fall, knocking over others and destroying valuable merchandise. A robot not properly in its place could fall over and demolish the rest of their scanty labor force.

In the interest of speed, Larramac offered to make Zhurat's check, but Dev vetoed that idea quickly. She knew only too well by now that her employer was a dilettante, more skilled at everything in his own mind than in reality. She performed the check herself, and only when she was satisfied that all was properly sealed away did she begin checking out the ship's routine functions.

Now, with all in readiness, the five people aboard were strapped into their acceleration couches in the control room. Dev was seated dead center, the console before her a maze of blinking lights, tiny switches, sensitive dials, and computer miniscreens for data readout. To her left was Lian Bakori, feeding data into his own computer banks with fingers moving so swiftly even Dev had a hard time following them. To her right was Gros Dunnis. The big engineer moved with more deliberate speed, but Dev refused to rush him. He knew his job; each move he made was exact, with no wasted effort. *Everyone works at his own pace,* she thought. *Rushing him would lead to mistakes, and we'd lose time while he did the job over again.*

At the extreme left sat Larramac, bored by the efforts of his crew and anxious to be underway. At the extreme right sat Grgat, strapped into the couch that had formerly been used by Zhurat. The native's eyes were wide with wonder at the totally alien surroundings. The purposefulness of the crew only made him feel more apart from the humans, but the mysteries that were taking place all around him gave him little time to dwell on his miseries.

At last Dev was satisfied that the ship was ready. Turning to their Daschamese observer, she said, "In a couple of minutes, Grgat, it's going to feel as though another person is sitting on top of you. You'll weigh twice as much as you do now, but it's only for a little while and after that you'll weigh nothing at all. It'll feel like you're floating. All set?"

The native grunted in response, which Dev took to be assent.

The digital clock on the console in front of her wound inexorably down to the moment of lift-off. Dev counted off the final ten seconds aloud, then—in conjunction with Dunnis—flicked the appropriate switches. The additional feeling of weight came instantaneously.

It was one of the paradoxes of physics that, in order to build up and maintain an antigravitational field outside the ship, the internal gravitation had to be increased by a corresponding amount. Custom was to lift off at an acceleration exactly equal and opposite to that of the planet they were on, requiring a rate of minus two planetary g's, or pg's—one to counter the planet's own pull exactly and one to thrust against it. Other factors entered into the calculations as well, most notably the velocity vector contributed by the planet's own rotation, which Bakori had to compute as a function of launch-site latitude. Once in the air, the ship was subject to buffeting from unpredictable winds;

70

Dev had to focus her full attention on the instruments to keep their course true.

Despite her warning to Grgat, the extra weight still shocked him. He moaned slightly and trembled as he was pressed deeper against the springs of his couch, but he said not a word; having resolved to undertake this venture, he did not want to appear a coward now that the point of no return had been passed.

There was little noise thoughout the ship as it rose with seeming effortlessness off the Daschamese plain, except for Grgat's mild whimperings and the slight unavoidable vibrations in the walls. The quiet was deceptive, though. The forces involved in lifting them off the ground were among the most powerful known to man—which was why Larramac could consider using the drive as a weapon against the gods.

At last Bakori, monitoring his instruments, announced that a satisfactory orbit had been attained. Dev gave a brief nod and reached out to kill the power of the gravitic drive.

The effect was instantaneous. The interior gravity shut down and the crew found itself weightless. To the humans, this was entirely routine; all were veterans of countless previous space flights and knew what to expect. But the abrupt switch from too much weight to none at all was more than Grgat could handle. All of a sudden he felt himself falling, and he twisted wildly around on the couch trying to steady himself. He ended up digging his paws deeply into the padded leather of the seat, hugging it to his chest for all it was worth.

Dev quickly finished up her immediate duties and turned to the frightened native. "Relax, Grgat," she said into the translator. "This is perfectly normal in space. It's called freefall, and it takes a little while to get used to. Once you get accustomed to weightlessness, you'll be able to move around freely like this."

To demonstrate, she floated out of her own couch and swam over to him upside down. The poor, stricken Daschamese saw her approaching at an impossible angle and shut his eyes to block out the dizzying sight. But it was too late; his sense of equilibrium—and his stomach—had already been offended. With a series of convulsions he began vomiting up his last meal.

Dev watched him react to this strange new environment. She felt compassion for the poor native and anger at her own stupidity. She should have realized how freefall would affect someone like Grgat, who'd never even heard of the concept before; she should have had the proper equipment right at hand. Granted, she'd had larger problems to occupy her mind, but she should have foreseen something as basic as this and been prepared for it.

"Roscil, get the vacsuck and clear this sludge out of the air before it gets into the filters." She could spare neither herself nor the two crewmen off the boards for very long until their holding orbit was laid in completely, so she felt no hesitancy about ordering around the man who was paying her salary—and Larramac, realizing the situation, obeyed promptly.

He can be so understanding when he wants to be, Dev thought exasperatedly. *Why does he have to be so drumheaded the rest of the time?*

She held onto Grgat's arm as long as the alien continued heaving. As soon as he was steady once more, she patted him lightly and returned to her own couch. She and Bakori checked their orbital parameters and made slight corrections; then she set the ship's trivision scanners at the widest possible angle and adjusted the radio receiver input controls. Behind her, Larramac re-entered the control room with the small suction device and was using it to pick the globules of Grgat's vomit out of the air.

With her task complete, Dev pushed herself gently away from the control board. "I've set our receivers to monitor a wide band of radio frequencies as we pass over the planet. At this altitude, we complete an orbit once every ninety-seven minutes and Dascham, of course, rotates under us during that time. I estimate it should take about five orbits before our sensors can scan all the area that Grgat might refer to as northeast."

She sketched on the mercator maps of Dascham the W-shaped projection of *Foxfire*'s path over the planet's surface. "We'll keep monitoring the instruments at all times. If the receiver dials show anything out of the ordinary, check the visuals on the screen and sound the alarm Bakori, you take watch the first two orbits; Roscil, you take the next two. I'll take the fifth orbit. If nothing shows by then, we'll consider alternate methods of detection."

"Can we afford to take all this time?" Larramac asked. "The gods will probably be monitoring us, and they'll see that we're not disappearing into hyperspace as we should. Won't they worry about us?"

"Let them," Dev said wearily. "Why shouldn't gods worry about mortals every so often? Do their souls good, I think. As for myself, I'd like to have at least a *little* bit of rest before we begin our attempted deicide. Things will get very busy very quickly, and I'd prefer to cope with it with a clear mind. Dunnis, I'd like you to get some rest, too—you didn't get that much last night."

She swam to the back of the cabin and was out the door before Larramac could say much to stop her. Nothing short of the discovery of Mount Orrork would get her out of her cabin before her watch, she promised herself—and she fervently hoped the mountain would stay hidden a while longer.

Dev was so tired that, despite her problems, she fell right to sleep as soon as she was in her hammock. Her sleep lasted a full five and a half hours before her alarm woke her to get ready for her observation shift. After a hasty attempt to make herself look presentable she swam afore to the bridge. Larramac was standing watch, as she'd ordered; she relieved him a few minutes early and told him to get some rest. Strapping herself into her couch, she proceeded to keep her eyes on the dial that measured receiver input.

She had only been on watch a few minutes when she heard a slight sound behind her. She spared a second from the board to look over in the direction of the noise.

Grgat, who had been in Zhurat's cabin, was returning to the bridge now. The native was still not certain about his movements in freefall; he clutched at the walls and moved very slowly, as though each motion might well be his last. With infinite care he pulled himself forward to his acceleration couch and stretched out over it. He tried to strap himself in, but his hands were not adept at working the buckles.

Dev loosened her own straps, swam over quickly to help him fasten his, then returned to her own couch. The maneuver took less than ten seconds.

Grgat growled something at her. Without taking her eyes from the dial, Dev reached for her headset, put it on, and turned it to "Translate." "Please repeat, I didn't catch what you said."

"I said I must seem rather stupid to you, and very helpless."

"Not at all. For someone who'd never even heard of freefall until just a few hours ago, you're doing fine."

"I owe you many thanks for your kind treatment. You had the right to kill me when I stowed away, I suppose, but you didn't. You refused to hand me over to the gods, and now you're willing to fight them for my sake."

Two out of three isn't bad, Dev thought, but said nothing.

"You're not afraid of the gods, are you?" Grgat asked.

"Not exactly afraid. Let's say I respect them, like I respect a knife or a dangerous animal. They have the power to do great damage, or even kill me. It's all a question of how you handle them."

"And you do not fear the demons either." It was more a statement than a question.

"I don't know, I've never met any. I prefer to reserve my judgment until the need arises."

"What gods do humans believe in?"

Dev took a deep breath and let it out slowly. "You can take your pick. These days, most humans believe there is a mystic force spread through the Universe, a cosmic overbeing attuned to individual consciousness. It's personified as Space, because it is all around, and it can have whatever attributes one thinks are convenient at the time. Even within the ranks of the faithful there are divisions, though. Some people look at the basic

74

natural laws and say that Space imposes order on the Universe. Others look at entropy—that is, the tendency for everything to wear down—and insist that Space opposes all attempts at order in subtle ways. And there are all variations in between.

"Then there are the minority religions. For example, Lian Bakori, our astrogator, is a Neo-Buddhist. He feels that the real world we see all around us is a hoax, that our souls dwell on another plane altogether. In order not to be duped by this hoax, they follow the principle of Minimal Involvement—that is, they try to have as little as possible to do with reality, in the hope that it will bring them closer to the state of *nirvana* which is a total escape from the hoax."

She smiled at the native. "It's nowhere near as clear cut and simple as you have it here on Dascham. In some ways, you should be grateful—you've never had religious wars, Crusades, jihads . . ."

"Which of these religions do you believe in?" Grgat asked.

Dev licked her lips. How could she explain the depth of philosophy in which she'd been raised to a native who, while far from stupid, was unsophisticated in such matters? Even the overwhelming majority of human beings misunderstood the regimen that governed Eos.

"I don't follow either of those beliefs," she began. "About two hundred and fifty years ago there was a philosopher who called himself Anthropos, which means 'man' in one of our ancient languages. It was his theory that it didn't matter whether there were external deities or not, because all humans—or actually, all thinking creatures—possess god within themselves. This was hardly an original thought with him; virtually all other religions have mentioned it in one way or another. But Anthropos was unique in the amount of stress he put on it.

"To Anthropos, what goes on inside a person's mind is far more important than anything else. A person who is at peace with himself will deal in a much more effective way with the Universe. A person must be 'sane'—in other words, he must consider all his actions, weigh all the possible consequences, and then take responsibility for them. It's not really a religion so much as a philosophy of life. We believe only in ourselves and what we experience. If we experience gods—as I did here—then we believe in them. If not, we keep an open mind until we do."

"I think I understand," Grgat said hesitantly.

"The basic theory is very simple," Dev said. "It's the practical application that usually gets out of hand. Anthropos' followers settled together on a planet named Eos to try to establish his policies in a full society. Within its own parameters it seems to work as well as any other system, but we have troubles when we mix with outsiders. Because we concentrate on the individual, and on each separate person's responsiblity, we're called self-centered, snobbish, superior . . ."

She broke off suddenly as the needles on the dial jumped alarmingly. She turned to the trivid screen and stared at the sight that was just coming into view. "There it is." There was no particular triumph in her voice, just a cool, matter-of-fact statement. With one hand, she reached over to record what the screen was scanning, while with the other she turned on the intercom so that it would be heard in all cabins throughout the ship.

"We are now passing over Mount Orrork," she announced like a tour guide calling out points of interest. "There can't be any mistaking it—it's all by itself down there." She switched off her intercom again, confident that Larramac, at least, would be in the control cabin within two minutes.

The ship's owner beat her prediction by nearly thirty seconds. Mount Orrork was still on the viewing screen, just passing out of the picture at the bottom. Larramac stared in unabashed amazement. The mountain was standing apart from anything else, not part of a chain, not even fitting into the general landscape. It was sticking out of a flat plain like a giant pimple on the face of Dascham. They could not estimate its height immediately from this angle, but it had to be at least a kilometer and a half across the base.

Larramac had not said a word since entering the room, so Dev chose to break the silence. "Of course, I can't be absolutely positive that's Orrork; the gods may be using other mountains as relay stations. . . ."

Larramac waved her technicalities aside. "That's it, I know it. My intuition says so."

"It's nice to see your intuition agreeing with mine for a change," Dev smiled.

Larramac noticed her facial expression and returned it. "You've got a nice smile, Dev. You should do it more often."

"Thanks. You should give me fewer problems and maybe I would." She turned back to the intercom and summoned the other two crewmen to the bridge.

Bakori and Dunnis were there within another five minutes and Dev replayed the scene of Mount Orrork passing beneath them. Bakori, as usual, was stoic, but Dunnis was quite impressed. "That's a big mountain. Are we going to attack that?"

"It's up to our boss," Dev said, and eyes swiveled to Larramac.

The gentleness that had been in the owner's face scant moments before vanished, replaced by a hard-edged greed that made Dev feel slightly queasy. "You drumming well bet we are," Larramac said. "A mountain's a mountain as far as I'm concerned."

I *take it you haven't met too many of them*, Dev thought, but kept the opinion strictly to herself. "All right, we have an orbit to figure. I've already set the mountain's planetary co-ordinates into the computer. Astrogator, I need a descent path that will take us tail down on top of it. I want to come in fast at a low approach angle, keeping the body of the planet between us and the mountain until the last possible moment. The less time they have in which to see us coming, the less chance they'll have to react. Another feature of the orbit: retrofire out of our present orbit should also come at a time when we're out of their line of sight. Can you do all of that?"

Bakori nodded. "It will just take some time, that is all."

"Fine, let's not hurry it. We'll make another complete orbit while you're doing the work. In the meantime, Engineer, I want every system working to perfection. They may try to lob a few bolts in our direction as we're coming in at them, and I want us to stand up to some heavy shaking, understood?"

"Understood, Captain." Dunnis nodded his large shaggy head and set to work checking out his systems.

Quiet reigned in the cabin. For the moment, Dev was out of a job; her only responsibility was to see that her two subordinates performed their functions adequately. When they finished giving her the answers, then her turn would come to put them into practice—and all their lives would hang in the balance. No one knew that better than she.

Finally Bakori announced that he had the required orbit all set into the ship's computer. Retrofire would be in sixteen minutes. Dunnis spoke up a few moments later, saying that this ship was in as good a shape as it ever would be.

Dev drew a deep breath and let it out slowly. She pressed her palms together in a prayerlike gesture and tucked them under her chin. Her eyes were closed as she drew upon some inner resources the others could not guess at. When she opened her eyes again and spread her hands out in front of her there was not a trace of shaking in the fingers and her eyes had a cold, calculating depth to them.

"If anyone has to use a bathroom," she intoned, "I suggest he do it now."

As it turned out, they all did.

"We'll be working under gravity conditions again," Dev informed Grgat when they reassembled in the control room. There were less than two minutes before the scheduled retrofire. "When landing tailfirst, we can't just go straight down, as we came straight up when we took off—the air would burn us up. Instead, we have to spiral around through the atmosphere under controlled flight, so that we slip in gradually. Do you understand?"

"I . . . I think so," the native said, but the hesitancy in his voice and the puzzled glaze in his eyes made Dev doubt his words.

"Well, never mind. Just take it from me that you'll weigh about as much as you normally do for a while."

"That will be a relief," the Daschamese muttered. He did not like freefall at all.

Dev watched the chronometer on the board in front of her tick off the seconds and, at the proper moment, hit the switch for retrofire. The internal acceleration was only about one pg, but nonetheless, after several hours of weightlessness, it was a heavy feeling, and most unpleasant.

Foxfire drifted slowly surfaceward. At first there was little for Dev to do; the ship was committed to its course and the atmosphere through which they were traveling was still so thin that there was no appreciable turbulence. But after twenty minutes they began encountering crosscurrents, and Dev's job of piloting truly began. It was a delicate business, keeping themselves upright while they fell with all the gracefulness of a rock.

Dev knew that Larramac, for all his boasting, would never have been able to manage this. No matter how skilled he was with an airplane, the aerodynamic differences between that and a spaceship were overwhelming. Planes had wings, and were designed to co-operate with air currents, using them for bouyancy. Spaceships were bullet-shaped, owing to the discovery that hyperspace was a viscous medium; they were streamlined to pass through hyperspace with minimal resistance, but merely tolerated atmospheric conditions. They were kept upright by gyros and, very occasionally, short blasts from side stabilizing jets.

Atmospheric maneuvering was something every ship's

captain hated, and yet was the most essential part of his duties. Any half-trained idiot with a skilled astrogator and engineer could guide a ship through hyperspace. But landing well was an art that comparatively few could master.

As her hands played across the control console largely by feel, Dev kept her eyes on her instruments—particularly the chronometer. They were fast approaching the point where they would come over Orrork's horizon and be spotted by the gods. From that point on, they would be in constant danger, a target moving ever closer to the barrel of unknown weapons.

"Horizon point," she announced at last. "They now have a direct line of fire to us if they want, and we have nothing to return to them for eight and a half minutes. They'll be close enough then to get the effects of our backwash. We can only hope they're too astonished to act in the meantime."

As the sound of her voice died away, a silence descended on the control room. Dev's hands stayed near the power switches. If the gods decided to take target practice, she wanted to be ready to move in any convenient direction—most particularly upward. Regardless of Larramac's bullying threats, she was prepared to run if the gods mounted a serious counterattack before *Foxfire* could bring its backwash into play. Let him fire her then—it would be infinitely preferable to dying in a smashed-up spacecraft. And maybe by that time Larramac would see how hopeless their fight really was and give up.

Mount Orrork, however, remained still. Time wound down past the four-minute mark, and still the gods failed to react. Every human in the control room, even Dev, was sweating, despite the comfortably cool temperature. Only Grgat did not seem visibly affected by the tension—but then, he might not fully appreciate the dangers of the situation.

They must have seen us coming, Dev knew. *They must have computed our orbit and know we'll be coming down on top of them. They use gravitic drives for their angels, so they know what our backwash can do. Why are they waiting?*

Of course, it was possible that Larramac was right, that they simply knew they had no weapons capable of defending against a spaceship. But even if the gods were descendants of a defeated army in a space war, the first thing they would have done upon establishing a base would be to ensure their own defense against future attacks; subjugation of the natives would have had a much lower priority.

Perhaps time was a factor. If the gods had been here long enough, they might have dismantled their defenses when it became obvious they were no longer needed. Or the weapons might have failed after such a long period of disuse; perhaps even now the gods were desperately shooting at *Foxfire* with no result.

Dev could not allow herself to hope for that, though. After all, the gods were not sure what weapons *Foxfire* itself had; the most likely explanation was that they were holding their fire until they were positive they could achieve a direct hit on their first shot. It was not a comforting thought.

The war of nerves ground inexorably down to the crucial moment. "One minute to passover point," Dev announced. "Be prepared for a bumpy flight."

They were close enough that they could make out details on the mountain. It looked more like a volcano to Dev than anything else, being conical and tapering evenly to a peak. There was no sign of a crater or any volcanic activity, though, and the top of the mountain was covered with snow.

Near the summit, Dev could distinguish a small swarm of black shapes, occasionally reflecting a bit of the late afternoon sun. *The angels have all gathered for Armageddon,* Dev thought. *They know they'll be wiped out if they're still there in another minute, so they must have some plan in mind.* Her hands were poised over her controls, ready for anything.

The attack came in a single blinding instant. Flashes of light erupted from the mountainside, almost burning out Dev's eyes with their intensity. The captain moved quickly. First she used a short blast from her attitude jets to knock them slightly sideways; with her other hand she switched off the external cameras so that the screen in front of her went dead. She needed her eyes for work right now; she couldn't risk another blinding flash from the screen.

There was a loud boom that carried even through the walls of the ship. Concussion waves from the explosion rocked them from side to side, jarring them mightily. Dunnis cried out; it turned out that the shock had caused him to bite his own tongue, drawing blood.

That, at the moment, was a minor concern to Dev. *Foxfire* was now too close to the mountain to run away; the gods weren't just throwing firecrackers. The only chance they had was to follow through on their initial plan and hope they'd survive long enough to complete it. *Foxfire* had to swing over the mountain and kill those weapons with its backwash.

Her brief flare with the attitude jets had not seriously altered the ship's course, merely changed its tilt enough so that the blast would miss them. She had a second or two, at most, before the guns would reaim and fire again. She had to make sure *Foxfire* made as difficult a target as possible.

Her hands flew over the control panel. There was no time for her to think about what she was doing; every move had to be instinctive. Now the hours she had spent practicing and working at boards identical to this one came to the fore and her fingers took on a life of their own. Dials and switches yielded to her commands, causing the desired havoc.

The occupants of the ship felt themselves pressed into their seats with a force of three pg's as the ship suddenly zoomed upward. The shock wave from another mighty explosion rocked them and, at that same instant, Dev cut the gravitic field entirely. The ship, suddenly a dead weight, plummeted downward, just evading the next bolt of energy. Then Dev restored power at a reduced level of half a pg, and the fall slowed. The shot occurred below them this time.

Dev's evasive actions had saved them so far, but *Foxfire* engines had not been built to stand such a strain. As her fingers continued to work across the board, she found the response from the ship to be progressively more sluggish. *Foxfire* could not keep up with the speed at which she moved, and it was beginning an ominous vibration.

"Engineer, I need more control," she yelled, but Dunnis was having his own problems. The pain from his bitten tongue had taken his hands momentarily away from his own controls, and now, even though he was trying to keep up with Dev's maneuvers, he was slightly confused and two steps behind her.

There was another explosion, internal this time. Glancing over at the engineer's board while still trying to push her own into action, Dev could see that the number-three generator had blown, reducing their power by 30 per cent.

Her chronometer showed ten seconds until the pass-over point. If they could hold on at least that much longer, they would have a chance of taking out the big guns. But all her maneuvering had definitely affected their course by now, and with the screen turned off she could not check their progress. They might be flying too low, and simply crash into the mountainside. They might be too high, or off to one side, and their back-wash would miss the mountain altogether. Dev looked over to the astrogator's panel, but the numbers that were constantly changing on those readout screens seemed fuzzy and indistinct. Try as she would, she could not force her superactivated brain to interpret them in real-life terms.

She had only her pilot's instinct to guide her—and that instinct told her she was a shade too low, that the ship was just about to scrape the top edge of the peak. She flipped the switch for more power, hoping there was enough to obey this one last command. The internal gravity gripped them all and held them tight. Although the feeling was totally imaginary, it seemed she could feel the ship straining upward over the mountaintop.

The passover point was reached, and for a second there was silence. Dev blinked twice in rapid succession. "I think we may have—"

Then there was an explosion and everything went dark.

7

"A pessimist is merely someone who lacks the imagination to see the answer to his problem."
—Anthropos, *The Sane Mind*

Dev felt as though she and the ship had formed a cyborg unit; there was such a oneness between them that the sudden lack of power seemed almost like personal death. At the same instant, the artificial gravity departed, to be replaced by a weightless feeling in the pit of her stomach. This was not the honest freefall of space, but the very real sensation of falling. *Foxfire* was twisting and plummeting down toward a rendezvous with the hard surface of Daftscham.

She could not see, but that didn't mean she couldn't act. Ardeva Korrell had worked long and hard to excel at her job; she knew her board by feel. In an instant she had restored the drive, but it seemed to do little good. The ship plowed into the mountain with such a force that it overpowered the engines. Dev and the others were driven ahead with an impact that whipped their necks forward. Their bodies strained against the straps that held them, and Dev felt she was being cut in two by the restraining belt across her midsection. Air was forced from her lungs, and she lost consciousness temporarily.

Her thoughts as she came to again were muddy at first: a jumble of panic at the unknown situation she faced, and relief that she was still alive. The blackness around her was absolute, and she had to fight down the instinctive fear of blindness that threatened to overwhelm her. A memory from when she was four years old flashed back to her: she had awakened from a nightmare to find the room completely dark. She'd begun crying, which woke the other children in the dormitory and they began crying too. Even after the lights had been turned on, it took the dorm parents half an hour to calm the frightened children.

Oddly enough thinking of her old terror helped now to calm her mind. *I'm no longer a little girl fearing the unknown,* she reasoned. *True, I'm in more danger now than I was then, but I've got a weapon to fight it. A sane mind is the ultimate strength.*

Her breathing became more regular as she applied her mind to the current situation. The sense of sight was temporarily denied her, but she did have other senses. There was a feeling of gravity pulling on her, with the couch at her back being "downward." Yet from the way her body had been tossed upon the ship's impact with the mountain, they had crashed into it nose first. With the gravitic engines pushing them along, they should have wedged firmly in that position, so "down" *should* be in front of her, not in back. Unless . . .

She strained her ears to listen through the blackness. There were slight sounds of breathing around her, indicating that at least some of her companions had survived the crash. Beyond that, the ship was very still. She thought she could pick up a faint whining from the rear—a whining that would indicate the motors were still working. If that were true, it would explain the gravitational pull within the ship. No matter what their orientation was in relation to the outside Universe, the gravitic drive maintained its own orientation within the vessel. *Foxfire* could be balanced on the point of its nose for all Dev knew, but as long as the motors were going, "down" would continue to be the direction of the ship's tail.

The conclusion eased a few troubled spots within her mind. If there was still power to run the motors, then there would be power to take care of other systems as well. The fact that the lights had failed only meant that the main circuits had been burned out. There were backups that Dunnis should have been able to activate from his board—but everything had been so chaotic at that moment that Dev could hardly blame him for his failure. Dunnis was a competent engineer when allowed to work at his own pace; he just was not a man to be relied on instantly in an emergency.

"Is everybody else okay?" she called out.

At first there was no reply, but then a low moaning came from her right. "Dunnis, is that you?"

More indefinite noises, then a sharp gasp. "What? I . . . I can't see!"

"The lights are off," Dev answered quickly, trying to forestall her engineer's panic with a calm voice and a logical explanation. "The engines are working, though, so we at least have emergency power. Can you do something about switching to auxiliary?"

"I . . . I'm not sure. I can't see my board." Dunnis's voice was still edged with the faintest hysteria, his breathing still a trifle labored.

Dev unstrapped herself from her couch and got slowly to her feet. Her knees were still a bit shaky and she had to lean backward for a second to brace herself against the couch. When she was confident of her steadiness she took a step over to Dunnis's acceleration couch and placed a hand lightly on his shoulder.

"No reason to worry yourself," she said in gentle, approving tones. "You know what your board looks like, don't you? I bet you've seen it a million times."

"At least," Dunnis answered with a faint chuckle. Dev's soothing tone was having the desired effect; the residues of panic were deserting him.

"I'm not as familiar with your board as I am with my own, but as I recall the auxiliary internal systems switches are over on the right-hand side, aren't they?"

"Yeah, about halfway up, just over the dials that give the internal power readings."

"Good. Why don't you see if you can reach them and turn them on so we'll be able to see what we're doing in here?" The engineer hesitated, so Dev prodded a little harder. "Go ahead, reach out and try. Trust your hand—it probably knows the way better than your eyes do."

She could feel Dunnis leaning forward, slow and uncertain. There was the click of a tiny switch—and suddenly the room was filled with light.

Dev nearly cried out at the stabbing intensity after so many minutes in pitch blackness. She closed her lids tightly against the brilliance and knuckled at them slowly. After half a minute she felt more prepared to open them again, although they were still tearing copiously.

The right side of the control room seemed to be in good condition, but the left side was a mess. The wall of the ship there had buckled but not, apparently, split open. Larramac's acceleration couch, which had been at the far left, had been ripped out of its anchored position and knocked across the back wall to the other side; the ship's owner was still strapped in but unconscious, blood oozing slowly from a small gash along his left temple.

Lian Bakori was not quite so lucky. The buckling of the wall had occurred just in front of his position, knocking his control board forward into his body. Fortunately it had smashed downward against his left leg rather than into his abdomen, so the man would still live. But, from the way the console was pinned against him, Dev could guess that his leg was shattered—and she was certain that the astrogation controls had suffered a similiar fate.

Glancing back over to the right, she could see that Grgat also was out cold for the moment, leaving all the work up to herself and Dunnis. Fortunately, the engineer was large and muscular.

"Come on," Dev said to him. "Help me get Bakori out of that mess."

Working as gently as they could, the pair managed to slide Bakori out of his astrogation couch onto the floor. Despite their caution, it was a lucky thing the astrogator was unconscious. or their attempts to extricate his shattered leg would have had him shrieking in agony. As soon as he was free, Dev checked her boss. The cut on Larramac's temple was superficial, though it had bled profusely. Grgat showed no exterior signs of damage at all; shock and fright, Dev guessed, were what kept him unconscious.

Leaving Dunnis to watch over their patients momentarily, Dev went below to the small dispensary and took out the emergency first-aid kit. The ship was equipped with a medchest, which could do automatically almost anything a human doctor could; eventually, she knew, Bakori would have to be placed inside there to try to heal his smashed left leg. But right now, with the situation as uncertain as it was, she could not allow her astrogator that luxury. It might require several weeks to heal Bakori's leg—and they might not have those weeks to spare.

Returning to the bridge, she gave the astrogator a shot of painkiller; that would have to suffice for the present. Then she went over to Larramac and cleaned his wound. The owner's eyelashes began fluttering as Dev wrapped a bandage around the dressing. The man stared blankly ahead for several seconds before his full faculties returned. "How'd we do?" he asked his captain.

"No worse than second best," Dev replied crisply. "But we're still alive, which is a major consideration in itself. The ships is still functioning, though we're on auxiliary power for internal functions. Other than that, I haven't had time to check. I still won't for a little while."

Larramac blinked a couple of times, then held up one feeble hand. "Listen."

Dev did. "I don't hear anything," she said after several seconds.

"That's just it. No more explosions. They're not firing at us."

He had a point, though a slim one. "I haven't noticed them serving tea and cookies, either. At the moment I'm playing doctor; when I finish that I'll go back to my role of strategist."

She left her boss and returned to the more badly injured Bakori. With Dunnis's help she fashioned a crude splint and tied it onto the damaged leg. The astrogator had his eyes open, but the strong painkiller Dev had given him left the man quite doped up. She doubted he'd be fully aware of anything in the real world for several hours yet.

The fifth member of their party, Grgat, was still

unconscious. Dev didn't know what to do about him. Stimulants that would work on a human could conceivably kill a Daschamese. There might be some cathartic reaction within the Daschamese nervous system that made unconsciousness mandatory for recovery from shock. There simply was not enough information available about these natives for her to tell. She decided that, for the moment, she could let Grgat sleep; until she knew better what situation they were facing she did not need his help.

Now, though, came the moment she'd been dreading, and there was no way to put it off any further. "All right, Gros," she sighed, calling the engineer by his first name, "let's get to the bad news now. Pull me a complete status check on all shipboard systems so we'll know how we stand. As for myself, I'm taking a look outside."

She returned to her board and activated the trivid screen. Camera number one was not working; it was on the side of the ship that had gotten smashed in, and Dev expected it to be inoperative. With a great deal more nervousness than she allowed to show outwardly, she switched to a view from camera two.

The situation was as bad as she'd feared. *Foxfire* had crashed nose first into Mount Orrork, about halfway up the slope. The camera angle made it difficult to see, but from internal evidence Dev surmised that the one whole side of the ship was dented in. Even if they were pointed skyward, Dev would have hesitated to take off; she doubted that side would be airtight in any event.

Of course, they were not pointed skyward, and probably never would be. Their nose was firmly wedged into the rock and dirt that was Mount Orrork.

Foxfire would never leave the surface of Dascham.

She sat facing the screen for several minutes, letting alternatives drift peacefully through her head. There seemed little point in hurrying about anything any more.

Dunnis's voice cut through her reverie. "It doesn't look good, Captain. The engines are a major drain, but we can stay on auxiliary power indefinitely. Astrogation instruments are out almost totally—I guess you knew that—and so are most other computer functions. Life support is holding its own, but it's independent on everything. We've got two generators blown out—it might just be possible to repair them with what we've got on hand, but I can't promise anything."

"Don't bother," Dev said weakly, then forced herself out of her apathetic state. "What about the radio?"

"No problems there, but who are you going to call? The gods?"

Dev's lips twitched into a smile that vanished as rapidly as it appeared. "No, I think it's a bit late for prayers and atonement. Just thought I'd ask. I have to take everything into account."

She turned to Larramac, who had propped himself up on his elbows and was watching her with interest. She explained their situation to him as succinctly as possible. Larramac's face fell, and he looked as abashed as a little boy with his hand caught in the cookie jar.

He looked as though he were about to say something—possibly an apology—but Dev cut him short. "What we have to do now," she said, "is consider all our alternatives. Give me a few minutes to formulate my thoughts."

She turned back to the screen in front of her and, out of curiosity, switched to the view from camera number three. From the angle at which they were lying, this camera would be pointed uphill along the mountainside; perhaps it would give some indication of what the gods were doing while the humans sat here, trapped.

A swarm of dark shapes circled in the air above them. Increasing the magnification, Dev could see that they were the angels, about fifty of them, gliding through the sky like hawks waiting for their prey to make some slight mistake before commencing their fatal swoop. For a second, Dev wondered why they stayed so far away rather than attacking; with the concentration of powers at their disposal, they could probably crack *Foxfire*'s hull.

Then she realized the full situation. *Foxfire* was lying tail upward with the engines on. The backwash of the gravitic drive would still be operating. The angels were hovering probably just out of the effective field limits, waiting for an opening. If Dev were to shut off the engines, the angels would descend to finish the job they had begun earlier.

Letting that fact simmer in the back of her mind for the moment, Dev turned around to face Dunnis and Larramac once more. "We have two basic alternatives," she began. "The first is to sit here and wait for help. Human trading parties do come here occasionally, as we did; there may be another along within a few months, and we have enough supplies to last that long. We could ask them to pick us up."

"That's *assuming* they come by here before our supplies run out," Dunnis said gloomily. He avoided looking at Larramac.

"It's also assuming that the gods will *let* them rescue us," Dev added. "After our little adventure today, I doubt they'd take kindly to any trading parties that show up. They'd probably wait for the traders to land, then ambush them unexpectedly, without giving them the chance to defend themselves."

"We could radio them and warn them," the engineer said.

"That's why I asked about the radio," Dev nodded. "But again, that is only assuming the gods are willing. We were able to jam the broadcasts of their bugs; they could more than likely jam our broadcasts, too." She shook her head. "No, even if another trade group came in time, I don't think we could make contact with them."

"That eliminates your first alternative," Larramac said quietly. "It leaves only your second, Which is . . .?" Although his tone indicated he already knew, he gave her the courtesy of asking.

Dev sighed. "We proceed on with our attack. After our unprovoked assault we can expect no quarter from the gods; they've already given ample proof that they're an unforgiving lot. At the first opportunity they get, they'll try to finish us off."

"They've been quiet ever since our crash. Maybe

they think we're already dead," the ship's owner suggested.

Dev shook her head. "Sad to say, you're wrong. The heavenly hosts have been keeping us under constant surveillance. Admittedly, their big antispacecraft guns have been quiet. I can think of two possible reasons. One is, we may actually have succeeded in doing damage during our pass over the mountain, and they may no longer have that weapon at their disposal. The other is, we may be situated at an angle below their effective range. It wouldn't matter to them in the slightest whether we *might* be dead inside here; if they had the firepower they'd obliterate our ship just to make certain. The fact that we're not merely dust particles scattered over the face of the mountain proves they're at some disadvantage."

"A point for our side," Larramac commented.

"But a minor one. As I mentioned, the angels are circling up there. The only thing holding them at bay is the backwash of our drive, which is still on. As soon as we turn that off, they'll be swarming down here on top of us."

"But then we're trapped here." Dunnis protested. "We can't leave the ship while the field's on, or it'll burn us to a crisp as well. And if we can't leave here, we can't attack them back."

"That *is* a problem," Dev admitted, nodding her head slightly. "Not, however, an insoluble one. There are feints and diversions that can be carried out. If I assume for a minute that we can get out, the question then becomes, where do we go from there? And that, in turn, brings me to another question of equal importance."

She turned to face her employer squarely. "It's time to stop being coy, Roscil. You'd better tell me about those weapons you've got stashed down in the hold."

Larramac looked even more chagrined than before and cleared his throat self-consciously. "Yes, I, uh, had been going to get around to those. I originally only meant this trip to Dascham as a quick one-week stopover on our way to Brobinden. I don't know if you've ever heard of them, but they've got a war going on there."

"And you thought you'd just help them along, is that it?" Try as she would, Dev could not keep a glimmer of disgust out of her voice.

"Why not? I didn't start the war, but if they're determined to kill one another they'll do it whether I sell them weapons or not. Why shouldn't I make a profit on it?"

"Are you partial to one side, or will you sell to all parties equally?"

"Listen to who's talking!" Larramac roared back at her. "You Eoans always claim to be above morals, everyone knows that. You're so good you can do whatever you drumming well please."

"Is that what everyone knows?" Dev shouted back. "Well, everyone is wrong. We're not above morals, we're beyond them."

"I fail to see the difference."

The cleansing effect of anger had washed through her system, purging it of the bitter frustration she felt at the "death"—or at least fatal disability—of her ship. Yelling back at Larramac had done her some good, but she didn't want to be carried away by too much of a good thing. She put a clamp on her emotions once more and forced her voice into more even tones.

"The difference is subtle, but it's there. Anthropos saw morals as arbitrary rules imposed by Society on its less mature members—those who can't or won't think through to the consequences of their actions. A person who knows what he's doing, why he's doing it, and what the consequences are likely to be doesn't need morals as they are conventionally defined. What he *does* need is a set of social values and an appreciation of the delicate balance of human interactions."

Larramac snorted. "Damned Eoan double-talk. You're all very good at that, too."

"No, honestly," Dev said, shaking her head. "Listen. If I were to sell a gun to someone, I would have to think it through to the consequences. Guns really have only one function—to kill or injure. Therefore, I would have to take into consideration that—by selling this gun to this person—I could be contributing to the death of one or more people. I would have to weigh that very carefully. My customer may be concerned that someone will attempt to kill him, or he may be a criminal out to upset someone's social balance. My estimate of his intentions will have to play a part in my decision of whether to make the sale."

"But you admit there are some circumstances where it would be justified," Larramac said in triumph.

"Of course. There are some circumstances where any conceivable action is justified. Everybody has to have *some* set of values on which to guide their lives. Anthropos suggested that a balanced society is the goal to strive for. 'The sane mind functions best in a stable environment.' Peace, happiness, and rational behavior will make a culture more stable; war, misery, and irrationality destroy stability. Eoans are brought up to work for the first set and fight the second, if possible.

."If, for instance, I were in a society that looked peaceful, but remained that way by keeping most of its citizens in slavery, I might see it as my duty to join a revolutionary group and overthrow the established order. *But* I would think through the consequences of my action; if I were captured by the establishment, I should expect to be tortured and killed. I would be, in essence, beyond the law but still subject to it . . . and I would know that before I even began my course of action. I would . . ."

Dev broke off suddenly and looked at her audience of two. "I'm sorry, I didn't mean to sermonize. I guess the tension of the situation got to me." She looked back down at her feet. "I was talking about battle tactics before we drifted into irrelevancies. Those weapons in our hold—it doesn't matter what they were originally intended for, the fact remains that we need them now for our own purposes. How well armed are we?"

"We've got pistols, rifles, grenade launchers, personal energy cannons, belt deflectors, charge field generators—and, of course, plenty of power packs to keep them all supplied." Larramac was positively glib as he ran through the inventory of destructive potential.

"I suppose if the ship were a little bigger we could have managed a tank or two," Dev commented sardonically. "It's a shame—we really could have used one of those. Well, we'll have to go on foot. At least we'll be as well armed as any infantryman has a right to expect.

"Bakori will have to stay here. With his leg crushed that badly he'd be nothing but a liability outside. Besides, someone will have to stay here and keep things in order. The other three of us—no, four; we'll have to wake Grgat up somehow, he's got as much of a role to play in this as the rest of us. The four of us will have to go out and continue our assault somehow."

She looked back at the trivid screen, which showed the circling angels and the tip of Mount Orrork in one corner. "Four people," she muttered to herself. "Four people to go against fifty of those Avenging Teddy Bears and a mountainful of gods."

8

"If you can't achieve perfection in yourself, how can you expect it in others?"

—Anthropos, *The Sane Mind*

It took Dev ten minutes to rouse Grgat from his involuntary hibernation while Dunnis and Larramac went down to the hold to unpack the weaponry. Dev tried shaking the bulky native first, and when that failed to produce results she tried light slaps across the side of his muzzle. His eyelids fluttered in response, until finally he was looking at her. It took perhaps half a minute more for awareness to seep into his brain that he was still alive, and not sharing with these strangers whatever afterlife he believed in.

"Are you all right?" Dev asked him through the translator.

Grgat was slow to answer, but did so in the affirmative. He tried stretching his arms and legs, finding them stiff but workable. Dev unstrapped him and he rolled off his couch to stand uncertainly on the floor of the bridge.

Quickly, she filled him in on their situation, that they had crashed onto the side of Mount Orrork and that, while temporarily safe, they had no alternative but to continue their attack on foot. They were as well-armed as humans could expect; everything now depended on the size and versatility of the gods' forces.

Bakori was still unconscious. Dev left the native to watch over her astrogator, with instructions to call for her if the man showed signs of returning to awareness, then went down into the galley. It had been hours since they'd all eaten, and Dev was positive that a meal would ease at least some of the strain under which they were working. She only wished her cooking skill was as good as the situation required.

She completed her chore at about the same time Larramac and Dunnis finished uncrating the weapons. She called them up for dinner and, while they attacked their food ravenously, she brought a serving up to Grgat on the bridge.

The Daschamese thanked her and ate slowly despite a great hunger. The human food was still strange to his palate, and he seemed to contemplate every bite. But Dev could tell that there was more on his mind than just food.

"We're doomed, aren't we?" the native said at last.

Dev smiled, even though she knew he might not be able to read the gesture properly. "You have to have a little more faith than that."

"I did have faith—in the gods. I've seen what they can do. Killing my wife weakened my faith in them, and I turned instead to you humans. Now you have failed me, too. I don't know what to believe in." He gave a brief snort. "Besides, you were telling me not long ago that it was your religion that had no steady faith."

"No, I never said that. Faith is the cornerstone for the actions of all intelligent beings. We Eoans choose to believe in ourselves rather than in externals, that's all. I know pretty well how strong I am, how fast I am, how smart I am. I know my own particular skills, and I know my own weaknesses. I plan my actions around these things, but I always maintain my faith in my own abilities. In a universe of changes, I'm the only constant I can be sure of.

"We don't believe in proselytizing very much, for the simple reason that ours is a hard discipline to follow for anyone not raised in it since birth. It's better, in many cases, not to even start than to get halfway into our philosophy and then suddenly find oneself floundering. So I want you to believe that I'm not trying to convert you when I suggest that you try having faith in yourself above all.

"You saw what happened when you left your faith in

the hands of other people—they either abused it or let you down. Believe in yourself first, and you may be less disappointed in life. Faith *can* work miracles, if you apply it correctly."

She stood up and walked to the back door of the cabin. "And speaking of working miracles, I've got to get back to our other two friends and help them plan our campaign." She left the native still thinking over her words.

Arriving back at the galley, she found Larramac and Dunnis in the midst of an argument about their future tactics. "But you can't just walk up the hillside," the engineer was saying. "I've seen what those angels can do. They're accurate with those lightning bolts at better than a hundred meters."

"But we have guns, too," the ship's owner countered. "They'll be more ready to keep their distance after we've picked some of them off." He saw Dev enter and turned to her for confirmation. "Isn't that right?"

"Perhaps. Although there's more than fifty of those Teddy Bears and four of us; a concerted suicide charge would wipe us out, if they have the chance to make one." She glanced over at Dunnis. "But we will have to climb the mountain somehow despite the risks. We'll need tactics that will maximize their hesitancy to attack us and minimize their efficiency."

Larramac leaned back in his seat and looked at her. "I presume, from the way you say that, that you have such a plan in mind."

"As a matter of fact, I do. Have you known me to be without one?"

"Sometimes I think you have too many."

"That's because I'm always changing and updating them. In this case, in addition to our own weapons we have two factors operating in our favor. One is that the angels can't make an effective suicide charge—they're powered by gravitic engines, and can't get too close to one another or they'll destroy themselves. They have to spread out in a wide configuration to operate without fear of mutual backwashing."

Dunnis pounded his forehead with his palm. "Why didn't I think of that?"

"You probably would have," Dev soothed. "It just occurred to me as I was speaking."

"You mentioned a second factor," Larramac prodded.

"Yes. I propose that we climb the mountain after dark. From what I've seen the slope is fairly even—no smooth faces or escarpments to give us special trouble. It'll be harder than in the daylight, but it will also be safer as far as going undetected."

Dunnis was shaking his head. "Sorry, Captain, but that won't work. It was pitch black and pouring rain when that angel blasted Zhurat into a small pile of ashes. They've got special sensors to take care of that problem."

"The special sensors that they have are their bugs. We know they spaced them every few meters in the village. Zhurat was yelling at the top of his lungs; it would have been simplicity itself to triangulate his location with respect to the various bugs and aim, not at him, but at his position.

"The situation here is quite different. According to our maps, there are no native settlements within five hundred kilometers of this mountain. Even though the gods believe in being thorough, even though they have almost unlimited resources to draw on—even so, putting bugs on the side of their own mountain, when no one ever comes near it, would be a complete and utter waste of time and materials. I'm willing to stake my life on the assumption there are no bugs—at least, no electronic ones—on the mountainside."

"What about searchlights, though?" Dunnis persisted. "Surely they would have those to illuminate their mountain in case of trouble."

Dev nodded slowly. "Yes, we'll have to deal with those. We have little alternative but to fire directly into the light and hope to knock out the source. If we can get ourselves into an entrenched position first, we might stand a bit of a chance. Don't forget, by turning on the lights, they also make themselves visible to us—and their big tactic is surprise; they like to launch their lightning from out of nowhere and then claim the credit for it afterward. If we can see them, too, we're well enough armed to keep them at a distance.

"Once they realize that, they'll keep their lights out most of the time. If we proceed with relatively little noise, they won't be able to get a fix on us—and hopefully, we'll be able to climb in peace."

"Sounds good to me," Larramac said.

Dev nodded curtly. She had not listed the disadvantages of her plan—the largest one being that none of them were, as far as she knew, experienced mountain climbers. Her own knowledge of mountaineering was entirely theoretical—she'd read a few microspools on the subject some years ago, but that was all. She was asking a team of four untrained people to make the climb in the dark in almost complete silence. Part of the climb would be through snow and ice, always treacherous conditions. And, once they made it to the summit, they had not the faintest idea of what they would find. The gods' fortifications were still an unknown quantity; they could make it all the way to the top and then fall victim to some deadly force field none of them had suspected.

Dev gave a mental shrug. If the game was worth playing at all, it was worth playing to win. She could but do her best and hope it was enough.

"You still haven't told us how we're going to get out of the ship," Dunnis said. "We can't leave while the drive's on, or we'll be killed—and if we turn the drive off, the angels will come down and blast the ship before we can make our move."

"All in good time," Dev said mysteriously. "There are plenty of preparations to be made first."

Bakori returned to consciousness several hours later, although he was in considerable pain. Dev performed the job once more of giving him a status report, and Bakori accepted it with his usual calm unconcern.

"We'll get you into the medchest to take care of that leg, but there'll be a few things you'll do for us first," she told him.

Then she went down into the hold and inspected the weapons Larramac and Dunnis had uncrated. "We'll all take belt deflectors and hope they can handle what the angels will throw at us," she decided. "Everyone will have a pistol and a rifle. I don't think we can expect Grgat to master anything more complicated than that. Roscil, you and I will carry grenade launchers as well; Gros, as the biggest of us, you can haul the cannon around."

"They're not too cumbersome," Larramac said. "Why don't we each carry one? It'll increase our firepower tremendously."

"We're making a forced climb up a very steep grade under the ever-present threat of attack," Dev explained patiently. "After a couple of hours, every gram you're carrying is going to feel like a kilo. I want to keep our configuration as simple as possible, and I'm willing to trade off some firepower to do it."

She took Grgat down into the hold and explained the use of the laser rifle and laser pistol to him. Their cargo was now totally useless—even Larramac conceded that— so Dev allowed the native to use the boxes for target practice. After several hours of burning up everything in sight, the Daschamese did get the hang of it; he'd at least be able to hit something the size of an angel if it was not too far away.

Of course, if the angels weren't too far away the *Foxfire* crew's chances of survival were not good; but Dev pushed that thought to the back of her mind. This was not the time for needless doubts; she dared worry only about those things she could control.

The rest of the team took target practice with pistols and rifles too, although they were already familiar enough with weapons to get by. The grenade launchers and energy cannon were another matter altogether, and could scarcely be tested indoors. Dev and the men contented themselves with reading over the instructions carefully and assuring themselves they knew how to operate the devices in theory.

They had two more meals and rested. It was late afternoon of the next day when they assembled again on the bridge. "I'm going to try to reduce the odds against us and make the angels a little more cautious at the same time," Dev said. "To do that, I'm going to have to turn off the drive for a brief period of time.

"As soon as the drive is off, we'll be subject to Dascham's normal field—and we're tilted at an angle toward that side. You'd better brace yourselves over there and be prepared for that side to suddenly become the floor."

"That's difficult for me," Bakori said, looking down at his mangled leg.

"Let's strap you into Grgat's acceleration couch, then. You'll feel like you're falling, which may cause some pain, but the straps will keep you from any real damage."

With Dunnis's help she tied the astrogator down to the indicated couch and waited until the others were all braced against the left wall. She herself was strapped into her own couch. Her right hand was poised over the drive controls while her left reached out to brace herself against the astrogation panel. Her eyes were focused tightly on the external trivid screen, which showed the full complement of angels still hovering above them.

"Everybody ready?" she asked.

The others all gave their assent.

With a decisive motion, Dev turned off both the drive and the internal antigrav field.

The effect was instantaneous. One moment the floor seemed solidly beneath her, the next it shifted violently over to the left. Dev's straps cut deeply into her as her body was pulled hard to the side. Even though the others in the cabin had been braced for the effect they too felt the jolt as Dascham's gravity reasserted its dominanace over them.

From the back of the ship came an ungodly crashing, and Dev winced. All the unsecured items in cupboards and on shelves would be toppling over to the left. *Space! Probably everything that wasn't broken in the initial crash has broken now,* she thought. *Why didn't I think to nail stuff down?*

But she had little time for recriminations. There was

movement on the screen before her. The angels were circling in, aware that the drive had suddenly been cut off. Some of them zoomed lower, aiming for the kill. Some others held back, wanting to make sure this was not a trap. The majority took a middle position, awaiting developments.

Dev watched nervously, her hand poised over the drive controls. There were several factors she had to evaluate, such as how many angels it would take in combination to deal a lethal blow to the ship, and what their effective range might be. Both could only be rough guesses, but she would have to wait as long as possible to get the maximum advantage from her ruse.

Finally, when even her nerves could stand the suspense no longer, she turned the drive back on. Instantly she was yanked back to her previous position, and "down" seemed right again. She had not been able to give adequate warning to her fellows, however, and they fell forward onto their faces with the new gravity shift. Below them, there was more crashing as the debris from the last shift slid around once again.

But it was the screen before her that showed the major effects of her action. The angels that had been the most eager to descend toward the ship exploded in a cataclysm of fire. The people inside the ship could hear small pinging sounds as bits of metal rained down upon the hull from the devastated robots.

Some of the robots who had not descended quite as far tried to lift upward out of the field before it was too late. They were not close enough to bear the full brunt of the gravitic field's fury, but they had gone too low to escape its effects. Their internal circuits shorted and blew out, leaving them just inert masses of metal. They fell like dead weights from their lofty height, and then exploded as they fell deeper into the backwash.

Dev made a fast count of the remaining angels. Fourteen still floated out of the field's effective range. With two quick flicks of her fingers she had significantly reduced the numbers of their opposition. Unfortunately, it would not be that simple a second time.

Still, she thought, *it'll give them something to think about.*

"Now we're only outnumbered three-and-a-half to one," she announced. "The rest of the angels have fallen."

"Great!" Larramac shouted. "That was a good trick. Now they won't rush us the next time we turn off the drive, so we can run out and take cover on the mountainside."

"Not quite right," Dev pointed out. "The instant they see us leave the ship they'll zoom in. They know that no one on board would turn on the drive again until we're safely out of range, which would give them enough time to kill us. We'll have to pull another feint first—but we'll wait until nightfall to try that move."

When the time came, Dev was once again strapped into her couch. All things were as they had been earlier that day, with the exception of Dunnis. Instead of being on the bridge, the big engineer was down by the outer door of the cargo hold with two of the robots.

"Here we go again," Dev announced over the intercom, and once more the drive was turned off. The jolting sensations were felt again inside the ship. Overhead, the fourteen angels continued to circle warily; they were not about to be suckered in a second time.

"Now, Gros," Dev called out. Below, they could hear a rasping sound as the cargo door slid noisily open. The two robots, dressed up in spare spacer uniforms, would now be racing out of the ship toward the cover of the rocks two hundred meters away. From the distance at which the angels were observing, it would be impossible to tell that those figures weren't humans. Some of the gods' machines would have to descend, either to blast them or to determine for certain that they were merely robots like themselves. In either case, Dev would be able to turn on the drive and destroy another angel or two.

She watched her screen anxiously. The angels continued to hover at the same altitude. One of them detached itself from formation to fly over the fugitives for a moment, but then broke off the chase and returned to its group. It was totally disinterested.

Dev was stunned. The angels had seen the decoys, and yet had failed to act. They had refused to take the bait. Somehow they had spotted her trick—but how?

After five minutes of watching the screens produced no further results, Dev reluctantly ordered Dunnis to close the hatch. With that done, she turned on the drive once more.

She wanted to avoid looking at Larramac as she got off her acceleration couch, but she knew she had to. The expression on her boss's face was one of superiority. "So, for once your plan didn't work right, did it?" he said. He sounded almost gleeful about her failure.

He has the right to gloat, she reminded herself sternly. *I've been setting myself up as the ultimate authority, and I've just been proved wrong.* "I guess not," she said aloud.

Larramac waited, the smile tight across his face.

"I made a mistake," Dev went on. "Is that what you wanted to hear?"

"I just wanted to see if you could admit it."

"I hope it gives you some comfort," she said, keeping her voice deliberate and unemotional. "Actually, I make mistakes all the time; I just try to catch them and correct them before anyone notices. Letting your mistakes hang out in public when they don't have to is sloppy and inefficient." She paused. "But this time I failed big, and I have no idea why."

"So what do we do now?"

"I don't know." Dev shook her head. "I know one thing we don't do, however, and that's to set so much as a single foot outside this ship until we know precisely why my ruse failed. I'm in no mood for suicide."

Dev went to her cabin and lay back on her cot. Normally she found the ceiling a good screen on which to project her thoughts, but tonight it looked merely like a blank bulkhead. The angels' reaction would be logical if they had not spotted the escaping robots; they wouldn't have risked another trap like the first merely to blast the ship. But they *had* seen the robots running away, had even tracked them a short distance before giving up the chase as a decoy. Somehow, the angels were able to distinguish between a robot and a human. But how?

Maybe their eyesight was more acute than she had estimated, or maybe the angels had ears sensitive enough to pick out the minute metallic sounds made by the machines. Both hypotheses seemed wrong to her, but she could think of no alternative that made any more sense.

With her mind no more satisfied than at the beginning, Dev allowed herself to fall into a fitful sleep that was troubled by dreams of being chased by an Avenging Teddy Bear with a flaming sword.

With morning came light, but no enlightenment. Dev went down to the galley and found, to her pleasant surprise, that Dunnis had already fixed breakfast. "You've been doing the meals too often lately, Captain," he said. "I thought I'd give you a little rest."

"Thank you, Gros." She smiled at him. "I think I may make a good ship's officer of you yet." The food was as bad as usual; Dunnis was no chef. But Dev refused to be daunted. "You're improving, too; maybe you'll turn into a good cook as well."

Her engineer beamed, and Dev let her smile echo his. *A good captain must know when to encourage her crew as well as discipline them,* she knew.

The warm feelings within the galley were broken in another moment, though, as Larramac entered. "I've been thinking about the angel problem all night," he admitted, "but I'm as much in the dark as I was before. Have you had any luck?"

Something in her boss's phrasing clicked over in Dev's mind. In the dark—of couse. The angels had seen the robots running in the dark, and they hadn't turned on any searchlights. They could distinguish between robot and human in the dark.

"As a matter of fact," Dev said offhandedly, hiding her excitement well, "I have. I know where I went wrong in my assumptions."

Larramac looked at her. "Well, don't just sit there grinning at me. What was it?"

Dev hadn't realized she'd been grinning. She wiped the expression off her face quickly. "Infrared," she explained. "There wasn't any light out there, yet they were able to determine that two shapes were running away from the ship, and that those two shapes were not people. What they detected was the heat being given off from the robots—and since the robots are at a different temperature from humans, they knew it couldn't be any of us."

Larramac paused to consider that, scratching thoughtfully at his goatee. "Sounds good, but how can we find out for certain?"

"We'll have to run another test tonight. This time we send out a robot with a heater so that it's radiating at thirty-seven Celsius. If they home in on that, we'll know that's what they're looking for." And all the while she was mentally cursing herself for not realizing last night that there were other wave lengths to the electromagnetic spectrum than just the visual.

"Assuming for the moment that they are picking up on the infrared," Dunnis interposed, "how will we get past them, or keep them from seeing us climbing the mountain? We can't very well turn off our bodies, can we?"

It was Dev's turn to dive into thought. "An infrared sensor doesn't just pick up heat," she mused aloud. "*Everything* gives off some heat. What it does is pick up temperature differences between a potential target and its surroundings. The robots were at a different temperature from the ground around them, but the temperature difference was not what would be expected if it were two humans running."

She drummed her fingers against the table top. "That leads to some interesting possibilities. Anything with a zero differential will be invisible to them in the dark. If we could lower our radiant temperature to the ambient temperature, they'd never spot us."

"In case you'd forgotten," Larramac said, "we're mammals, not some drumming reptiles. Our temperature stays at thirty-seven no matter what it's like outside."

"Internal temperature, yes," Dev agreed. "But I said *radiant* temperature, the amount of heat we give off. Our spacer uniforms are designed to hold in a good deal of that heat, keeping us warm in cold weather and in the vacuum of space. But it doesn't keep all the heat in; it lets enough out to prevent a fatal build-up. If we could prevent any heat loss—say, by stuffing our suits with insulation—and then chill the outside of the suits to ground temperature, the angels wouldn't be able to see us in the dark."

"You mentioned something about a 'fatal build-up' a moment ago. I don't like the sound of that."

"It'll get warm inside the suits, no doubt about that," Dev admitted. "Whether it'll reach lethal levels is problematical. But personally, I'd rather sweat a little than play catch with a lightning bolt."

"What about Grgat, though?" Dunnis asked. "He doesn't have a uniform. How will we keep the angels from spotting him?"

"Zhurat was about that same size. Maybe Grgat will fit into one of his spare uniforms. At any rate, it's worth a try."

They rounded up the native and helped him slip into one of their dead companion's extra uniforms. The fit was snug but acceptable, with the exception of the feet. The Daschamese were built with broad, flat feet which enabled them to walk better over the mud that was ubiquitous around the inhabited parts of the planet. Grgat found he had to curl his feet up slightly in order to fit them into the boot parts of the uniform.

"That's not good," Dev muttered. "We've got a lot of walking and climbing to do, and comfortable shoes are a necessity. A limping member of the team will hold us all back."

"My feet will not hurt," Grgat insisted anxiously. "My feet are very tough. I can make it, I know I can."

Dev hesitated. Grgat wanted to make himself useful, and was not facing reality with his boasts. Those boots could not be comfortable to someone with feet like his, and there was no way they could redesign the boots—they were an integral part of the uniform. Grgat simply would not be able to keep pace with the rest of them.

On the other hand, they were already terribly undermanned as it was. They would need every available gun if their assault was to stand a chance. Bakori was obviously out; to eliminate Grgat as well would leave them with a party of three—not a very formidable force.

Grgat saw her hesitation. "You told me to have faith in myself," he said. "Now I do. Cannot you have faith in me as well?"

"Snared by my own arguments," Dev laughed. "You did that very well; have you ever thought of being a logician?" At Grgat's blank look, she continued, "Never mind, it would be an unprofitable profession at this world's state of development. Yes, I can't very well deny you when you quote from such intelligent sources. You can come along. I only hope your feet don't suffer too badly."

There was no way of testing Dev's theory about infrared until after nightfall. In the meantime, they went around the ship ripping up blankets, cloth, anything they would be able to stuff inside their suits to act as insulation. Grgat in particular had fun shredding the material into pieces they could use. It was, at least, a game he could understand.

When darkness fell, they tried the decoy maneuver once again. This time, the robots dressed up in spacer uniforms had been heated to human body temperature. Dev paid close attention to her screen as the robots raced from the ship across the mountainside.

Two of the angels detached themselves from their formation and swooped down toward the fleeing figures. When they had reached a height of fifty meters the air around them crackled and those deadly lightning bolts lanced out to destroy the humans' machines.

At the same time, Dev reactivated the drive. The angels, unprepared for that move, were caught in the field and exploded instantly in a shower of fiery hot metal.

Two more gone, Dev thought, *bringing the odds down to three-to-one. Better, really, than I could have hoped for.*

But more importantly, she had proved her hypothesis that the angels were using infrared sensors. She now had the key to their abilities—and, she hoped, to her group's continued survival.

Now, she thought grimly, looking at those twelve black shapes on the screen that still hovered against the starry backdrop of Dascham's sky, *now the battle really begins.*

9

"A person can only feel alone if he's never gotten to know himself."

—Anthropos, *The Sane Mind*

It took almost two hours after that for them to get ready. Stuffing their uniforms with insulation proved to be a trickier process than they'd thought, and required more material than Dev's original estimate. The uniforms normally fit very loosely to allow their wearers flexibility, and all that room had to be accounted for. When they were finished they all looked quite plump and rounded.

I feel like an overstuffed scarecrow, Dev thought. The insulation had another disadvantage in that it weighed them down still further and hampered their freedom of movement. Bending their legs and arms was more difficult, and their speed would be affected. But invisibility, Dev decided, would be a better asset than speed; they would never be able to match the quickness of the angels' reflexes in any case.

With their padding all in place, they strapped oxygen tanks on their backs and sealed their helmets into place. The suits would have to be completely closed, or heat would leak out through the top and give them away—and that in turn meant that they would have to carry spare oxygen along with them, burdening them down still further.

Each of the climbers had a belt deflector with a laser pistol tucked inside it and a rifle strapped over the shoulders. In addition, Dev and Larramac also carried the blunt-nosed grenade launchers while Dunnis toted a personal energy cannon. All their pockets were bulging with spare power packs for their weapons. Dev had a twenty-meter length of rope tied securely around her waist. And all of the humans had on their translator headsets so they could communicate with Grgat.

Just standing here with all this gear makes me feel tired already, Dev thought.

Now that they were all sealed up in their snug cocoons, she reached for the container of coolspray. This was kept on hand in case of fire in the cargo hold, but Dev had a more immediate use for it. She sprayed the misty substance over the outsides of their suits—except for their helmets—until the dials of their belts indicated the outside temperature was equal to the ground temperature of the mountainside. Then they got their robots ready and stood by the big door.

"All set," Dev said, touching her helmet to the intercom speaker and yelling as loudly as she could.

Up in the control room, Lian Bakori was strapped into the captain's couch, waiting for his cue to act. The trivid screen was focused on the mountainside where the invasion party would be running. Bakori's orders were to turn off the drive and wait. If he could see them running, he was to keep the drive off until they had gone at least three hundred meters from the ship; if he couldn't see them—which was more likely in the darkness—he was to wait five minutes, close the hatch by remote control, and then turn the drive back on to protect the ship from further attack by the angels and perhaps even destroy any who had ventured too close in the meantime.

The antigrav cut off abruptly, and the people in the hold were thrown momentarily off balance, even though they'd been expecting it. They recovered quickly, though, and started to work. Dunnis slid open the massive door and, when that was completed, the group surged forward. In addition to the four live members of the team there were seven of the robots running among them. More confusion for the enemy, Dev had decided—if the angels could see anything at all, they'd see a large cluster of bodies surging forward. And if they started target practice on the group, the odds were against their hitting anyone important on the first try.

The door was half a meter above the ground level.

They and the robots jumped down and began running straight ahead, in a direction perpendicular to the ship. They had to be as far away as they could in the allotted time, or the reactivation of the gravitic drive would fry them to cinders.

They could not see where they were running. Dascham had no moon, and the stars gave them little encouragement. They ran blindly, hoping to sense any major obstacles before they hit them. The ground underfoot was loosely packed, like damp sand or fine gravel, and provided treacherous footing, but at least the slope on which they moved was not very steep here. They moved at a pace that would have been considered a fast walk in daylight; under these conditions, it was a frightening speed.

The ship was no longer visible in the darkness behind them, and only the slight vibrations through the ground gave Dev any indication that her comrades were paralleling her course. The night was darker than she had remembered, but at least it was not raining here as it did in the inhabited portions of the planet. She was all too aware that there were angels overhead, even though they'd turned off their impressive phosphorescent glow. The memory of Zhurat being struck by the lightning blast echoed through her mind, and the knowledge that death could rain so suddenly out of the sky was an ache in her gut.

Oh well, at least it would be quick, she thought, and continued on.

The watch on her suit belt indicated that nearly four minutes had elasped since they had left the ship's cargo hold. They should soon be approaching the rocks she had reconnoitered on the trivid screen. It was a small cluster of boulders jutting out of the hillside— not enough to afford them any real protection against an all-out attack by the angels, but a landmark where they could gather themselves together out of range of the ship's gravitic field, to brace themselves and to launch their assault on the citadel.

She ran full tilt into the rocks. If her suit had not been so grossly overpadded she might have hurt herself; as it was she rebounded and lost her balance. She could feel herself slipping downhill as the gravel slid beneath her feet. Flailing her arms about, she felt them grabbed by two stronger arms, and she was pulled upward.

She could dimly make out the forms of Larramac and Dunnis yanking her behind the rocks with them, while Grgat stood beside them and watched. The robots had run on past, as per their orders. Their function as a decoy was over; the invasion party would now be totally on its own.

As soon as she regained her footing, Dev stood alongside her companions and gulped for breath. She had not realized she'd been exerting herself that much, but her lungs knew better. The insulation was working only too well—she could feel her entire body dripping with sweat. She lifted one gloved hand to wipe the perspiration off her forehead, and then realized that would be impossible with her helmet on.

It was almost time for Bakori to turn on the drive again. To take her mind momentarily off the condition of her body, she turned around to look in the direction where the ship had to be. There would be nothing to see; the energies connected with the gravitic drive were at the more extreme ends of the electromagnetic spectrum and completely invisible to the human eye, but . . .

Two explosions ripped through the night air. In the sky over their heads, a miniature fireworks display was in progress as a pair of bodies illuminated the dark. Two of the angels must have descended too low, and were caught by the reactivation of the gravitic field. Fiery fragments of their metallic bodies rained upon the mountainside, but none fell near the four invaders.

Ten to go, Dev smiled to herself. The odds were improving all the time. Why, this was practically a picnic.

If only the ants weren't so deadly.

She touched her helmet to Larramac's. "Time to start climbing," she said. "I'll go first for a short distance until I find another secure spot. You hold one end of this rope. If I give one tug, it means I'm in trouble and need help. Two tugs means everything is secure and the next man can come along. We go one at a time; those not climbing are to have their guns ready in case of trouble and to cover the climber. Understand?"

"Right." Larramac's voice sounded very far away through the double thickness of the two helmets. But this was the only way they dared communicate; broadcasting over their suit radios ran too great a risk of having the messages intercepted and tracked by the gods or their minions.

Satisfied that her instructions would be obeyed, Dev broke the connection and started her climb up the side of the mountain, playing out the rope behind her as she ascended. The slope was gentle at first, and she was able to climb along the loose rock at a steady, albeit slow, pace. Her body was bent forward, her knees were springy, and she kept her feet pointed forward for maximum comfort. Her eyes were becoming almost accustomed to the starlit darkness. Although she still couldn't see with any precision, she began to sense the presence of the rocks around her, and could even make out something of their size and shape.

I wonder if this is how blind people adapt to being sightless, she thought, her curiosity aroused despite the danger of the situation. She was still not comfortable with her inability to see; but by relaxing and letting the night overtake her—by actually allowing herself to *become* the darkness—the inky environment was less frightening than it could have been.

After climbing nearly fifteen meters, she came to an outcropping of rock. It was an overhang that she could not hope to scale in the darkness; she would have to find a path around it. But, in the meantime, it would serve as a good resting point for the team. Underneath this ledge of rock, they would hopefully be safe from the gaze of the angels.

She sat down with her back braced against the rock and gave two tugs on the rope. Nothing happened for half a minute, and then quite suddenly she suffered a pull that very nearly dislodged her from her position and sent her tumbling head over heels down the hillside. Whoever the second climber was, he was using the rope rather than his own strength to pull himself upward. Even had Dev managed to belay the rope securely that would not have been wise; with the line tied only around her own waist, the consequences could be fatal, both for her and for the other climber.

Instinctively she reached out, and her hand grabbed a good-sized boulder. Pulling herself over to it, she clung for her life while the tugging at her waist continued. She was glad her suit had the extra padding at this moment, for otherwise the rope would be biting through her flesh and causing a great deal of pain. As it was, there was only mild discomfort and the knowledge that, if she let go, she and the other climber would be in for a nasty fall.

Her arms were starting to feel the strain and she thought she would surely have to let go in another moment when the other climber reached her side. From his general size, she could tell instantly it was Dunnis—the biggest of the lot, naturally. He tapped her on the shoulder to acknowledge her. Instead of responding in kind, she simply untied the line from around her waist and fastened it, instead, around the engineer's. If the rest of the team was about to pull the same stunt, Dunnis would be able to cope with it far better than Dev. Besides, he had earned a lesson in mountaineering.

When she'd finished her tying, she touched her helmet to his. "Hold tight to this rock," she said and, when he complied, she gave two sharp tugs.

She could tell from Dunnis's reaction a moment later that the next man in line was committing the exact same mistake: using the line as his sole support. She kept in close contact with her engineer to make sure the big man was in no great danger of slipping—but at the same time, she allowed herself a smug little smile. *It isn't totally sane of me to enjoy his discomfort*, she thought, *but these are insane times and a little insanity may help me cope better.*

Soon they sensed Grgat's presence beside them. Dunnis wanted to untie the rope from himself and let the Daschamese pay the same price for his stupidity, but Dev was firmly against that. If it had been Larramac, she wouldn't have minded; but the native had not even the remotest experience at this sort of thing, and she was willing to excuse his action this one time. Dunnis, however, should have known better, and he was going to pay.

After the engineer had suffered through Larramac's pulling on it also, Dev retied the line around her own waist and touched helmets with each of the other three in turn. Her crisp lecture was the same in each case. "This rope is to be used for guidance only, to show you the route your predecessor has taken. It will not, re-peat, *not* support your weight. All it's likely to do is send both you and me tumbling down the mountain, possibly to our deaths—and the noise would certainly alert the angels to the fact that *something* is happening here. You'll have to rely on your own sense of balance and your own hand and toeholds—and your own mus-cle power—to get you along. Is that clear?"

They all assured her it was.

With that point settled, Dev set out again. She had to move laterally for about ten meters before she found a way around the lip of the rock overhang, and the climb upward was harder. She remembered the little bit she had read about mountain climbing, and let her legs do most of the work, pushing herself upward with the thighs and calves rather than trying to pull with the comparatively weaker arm muscles. Once, a foothold she had thought secure broke off as she pushed against it, and only quick reflexes enabled her to recover her balance before falling.

She felt like an insect crawling across the face of this mountain in the dark. She was only too aware of how exposed her position was, and how some giant fly swatter could smash her body to jelly against the rock. Looked at critically from her present perspective, her assumption of infrared invisibility was a very shaky one. Even now the angels could be hovering silently nearby, observing her timid progress and debating at what moment to loose the fateful lightning of their terrible swift swords.

Climb, she told herself sternly. *You've done enough thinking the past few days to last you a month. Let your body take over for a change. Just climb.*

The rifle slung over her shoulders started to be a nuisance as it banged repeatedly against her right side. There had been no way to pack it securely enough to keep it from swinging a bit and yet still be easily accessible in case of attack by the angels. The bumping sensation was not painful, but it was as distracting as a buzzing mosquito that refused to land.

The awkwardness of the padding became more and more evident. Scrambling over rocks and loose gravel had not required great dexterity, merely determination; but climbing a steep incline required greater freedom of movement, more co-ordination of the climbs. And every motion Dev made felt as though it were occurring under water. The blankets and cloth stuffed around her slowed her down, made her have to work that much harder to bend her elbows and knees.

The heat, too, was mounting inside her suit. She was sweating profusely, and the sweat was absorbed almost at once by the padding that pressed against her bare skin. The blankets quickly became soggy and oppressive, disgusting lumps of matter whose very touch on her flesh was repellent—and she could not escape that touch.

In the dark, she almost fell into the opening that she came across so suddenly. It seemed to be the mouth of a cave, though in the dark one blackness looked very like any other. She dared not turn on her helmet light to investigate it more closely, but it had a level floor on which she could sit and rest. Looking around, she decided this would be a good rendezvous point so she gave two tugs on the rope, indicating that the others should follow her upward.

She was delighted to discover that they were heeding her advice and not yanking on the line this time. She had no way of checking their progress however, and could only wait until Dunnis appeared as a black form in the darkness beside her. He touched his helmet to hers. "Did I do all right this time, teacher?"

Dev smiled, even though she knew he couldn't see her face. "B+ at least. Let's see how your classmates do."

While waiting for the other two to join them, Dev stood up and felt around a little through the cave on whose lip they were sitting. She hesitated to move around too much; with the heat building up so rapidly inside her suit, she didn't want to exert herself any more than was necessary. Still, she had not expected to find a cave in the mountainside, and it was worth at least a slight investigation.

She walked a couple of meters into its mouth, but found it totally dark. Here she was cut off from even the faint patches of starlight she'd grown accustomed to, and she was reluctant to go any further. For all she knew, there might be some animal living on this mountain that made this cave its home, and she had no need to make any more enemies.

She checked her watch, which told her it was just before midnight, local time. They still had a good long period of climbing ahead of them before daylight came. She didn't think they would make it all the way to the top in one night—certainly not at the rate they were traveling so far—which meant they would have to hide somewhere during the day before continuing their progress the next night. A cave like this would have been ideal for that purpose, but it was just too low on the mountain; they had to cover as much distance as they could tonight.

But if there was one cave, perhaps there would be another one higher up. It was something to hope for at least, she decided as she walked outside once more to join her companions.

Her thirst was beginning to become an obsession. There was a nipple inside her helmet and, by turning her head, she could take a small suck on the warm water in her suit's pack. The container held only slightly more than half a liter; the suit had not been designed for such extreme conditions. Dev took only a tiny swallow, and warned her fellow climbers not to waste their water too quickly—they still had a long trip ahead of them.

The expedition began to take on a quality of sameness. The pattern had been established, and they worked at it mechanically. Dev would take the lead until she found a safe spot on which they could rendezvous; then, one at a time, the others would follow her. The basic procedure, at least, quickly became routine for them.

The individual details of the climbs, however, did not. The higher up the mountain they went, the steeper the slope became and the harder the rocks underfoot. Making the trek into the darkness on unknown terrain became more and more terrifying. Each climber knew that even the slightest misstep would send him on a fatal fall, and none of his companions would be able to help in the slightest. Their pace slowed consistently as each climber tested his footholds with extreme caution before committing himself a step further.

The heat was another factor that contributed to their slowness. All of them were now soaked completely through in perspiration. They felt as though they were swimming in their own sweat. Droplets trickled down the humans' foreheads and into their eyes, burning them, and they had no way to wipe them clean. They were going most of the way with their eyes closed now to prevent the salty liquid from trickling in; fortunately, vision was not the most important of their senses at the moment, but it was still an unnatural feeling to climb up a steep mountainside with their eyes closed.

They came to another cave, and Dev was sorely tempted to call a halt to this night's activities. Every movement was a strain now, and the atmosphere within her suit was so charged with her own sweat that she found herself breathing mostly through her mouth. Their first set of oxygen tanks was about to give out, so they took the time to change over to a new set and buried the empties behind some rocks so the angels wouldn't spot them in daylight. The change of air made no difference, though; the inside of Dev's suit still stank of her own perspiration mingled with the odor of soggy blankets.

As tempted as she was to stop at this cave, Dev decided against it. There were still three hours before dawn, and they needed to make as much headway as possible. With a sigh, Dev signaled that they were to move on.

Each reach, each step had become an act of self-torture. The rifle, grenade launcher, and spare oxygen tanks on her back had not seemed an unbearable load at first, but by now each item was a ton pulling on her shoulders. The soggy padding inside her suit next to her skin was like dragging around her own mass in dead seaweed. Her muscles shrieked in protest each time she raised an arm or leg to push herself one more little bit upward toward the gods at the summit. She gave up thinking altogether and put her body on automatic. Lift leg to next foothold, test its security; lift arm to new handhold, test its security; push upward with leg, groaning at the effort; reach stable position and gasp for breath; then repeat procedure with other arm and leg.

She had no way of knowing how far up the mountainside they had come. They hadn't reached snow level yet, but the snow was only at the very peak and she hadn't expected to reach that tonight. Snow and ice, of course, would present additional complications which she didn't even want to think about right now.

If this keeps up, she thought, *when we get to the top we'll be too tired to do anything but surrender.*

But if this climb was hard on her, she knew it must be agony for Grgat. The native was from a cold, damp climate, and the conditions inside his suit must be tropical now at the least. On top of that, his feet were crammed into boots that were much too small for the purpose. She could sense when he was with her that his walk had taken on a very mincing quality, and he sat or leaned against the cliffs as much as possible. Each step must be torture for him, yet he did not complain. Stoically he kept pace with the others. Dev admired his courage.

122

Dev found her muscles were becoming so fatigued that they would shake whenever she put any stress on them. At one point she found herself clinging to the face of the cliff in the same position for five minutes before trusting her body enough to press onward. She knew she would not be able to continue much longer without rest. The watch at her waist told her there was an hour yet before the first rays of light, but the sweat and the strain were becoming too much for her. She must find someplace to drop her weary body before it dropped down the mountainside.

Just as she thought that, she came upon the third cave. She couldn't believe her good fortune, nor did she try. The fact that the cave was there was enough for her; she could question the coincidence later.

Dunnis and Grgat had each managed to climb up to the cave with her, and Larramac was on his way. Dev leaned back and was just starting to relax when she felt a sharp tug at her waist. The rope pulled her forward toward the lip of the cave and who knew how much of a drop after that. Dev put out her hands and managed to grab hold of a rock at the very edge, or she would have been pulled right off her perch.

A voice came into her ears. "Help, I slipped! All I've got to hold onto now is the rope." Larramac was broadcasting his situation all over the mountainside via radio!

10

"Society is willing to exploit the responsible individual, but it rarely rewards him."

—Anthropos, *Sanity and Society*

For a moment Dev just lay there flat on her belly, trying to keep herself from being pulled off into empty space. She could not decide which was the worse calamity—having Larramac fall or having him use the radio. There was, of course, the chance that the angels were not monitoring that particular frequency—but it was not a likely chance. The angels had dealt with humans before, and they probably knew very well what wave lengths were standard for human broadcasting. At most, the party could count on a couple of minutes' safety before the angels zeroed in on their location, then they'd be in for the fight of their lives.

As long as radio silence was broken anyway, she saw little further harm in turning on her own radio. "Gros! Help me pull him up, fast!"

She felt the strong arms of the engineer pull her away from the sharp edge of the cliff. Dunnis was probably every bit as tired as she was, but he possessed reserves of strength she could barely have guessed at. Then there was more help as Grgat realized what was happening and added his strength to the effort. Within seconds, Dev herself was out of danger—but the problem with Larramac remained.

The three of them began hauling furiously at the rope, trying to pull t'eir companion up before the angels could reach them. Larramac would be a sitting target, dangling in open space at the end of the line, and the three of them would not be much better off. Their only hope would be to get the ship's owner onto their ledge and deep enough into the cave that the angels would have trouble finding them.

The rope scraped along the ground. Larramac and all his equipment were providing a downward tug of better than a hundred kilograms, and every milligram of that was concentrated at one point—the lip of the cave, where the rope went over the side. In Dev's mind she could imagine the line being abraded down to a single thin strand, which could snap abruptly and send her employer tumbling down the mountain to his death. She redoubled her efforts and ignored the protests of her muscles that they could perform no such functions.

Suddenly the line seemed to go slack. The thought flashed through her mind that her worst fears had been realized; but then she was aware that Larramac had made it to the edge of the cave and lifted himself up into it. They were all safe for the moment—but it would be a short moment unless they moved deeper into the opening.

"Take cover, quick!" she called, and moved to follow her own advice. Her legs had other ideas, however. As soon as she got to her feet to run, they collapsed under her, leaving her a limp and gasping pile on the ground. *All right, if I can't run I'll crawl,* she thought. *Who cares about pride at a time like this?*

Moving on her hands and knees, she scrambled forward into the mouth of the cave. She could feel the vibrations in the ground as her companions also took cover as quickly as they could. Her hair was stringy from the sweat, and perspiration was dripping down her forehead once more, so she closed her eyes. . . .

Even with the lids shut tightly she could see the sudden burst of light that hit without warning, and through her helmet she could hear the crackling of the air currents. The angels had found them, and were starting to fling their lightning bolts. She was glad her eyes had been closed; after straining against the darkness for so long, a bolt as brilliant as that would have left her blind and helpless for minutes, and easy prey for the angels' fire.

The fact that she was still alive was quite encouraging, though she had no way of knowing whether everyone else in her party was as fortunate. She quickly slipped her rifle off her shoulder and turned around to face the entrance of the cave. She opened her eyes to just the narrowest slits—enough to see by, but sufficiently closed to cut down the glare of any future lightning bolts.

She was still on her hands and knees. She could sense the presence of a living, moving body next to her—Grgat, it seemed like—and a laser beam shot by over her head, signifying that at least one other member of the group was alive and returning the angels' blasts.

Another lightning bolt answered the laser beam. Dev closed her eyes for a split second, then opened them again. In the faint afterglow she could see Larramac crouched up against the wall just barely out of the mouth of the cave—and, too, out of direct line range of the lightning bolts. He was fumbling with his own rifle, trying to get it into position to fire back at his attackers.

Dev thought she saw a dark form silhouetted against the cave mouth. Bringing her rifle up, she sighted quickly and fired. From behind her, Dunnis's rifle also shot forth a beam of concentrated light. Both rays hit target with a splash of ruby brilliance, lancing through the outer plates of the mechanical Teddy Bear. It attempted to fire back at them, but its circuits were damaged and the bolt struck spectacularly—but harmlessly—against the cave's left wall. Out of control now, the angel slipped down the mountainside with a loud series of crashes until it passed beyond the humans' hearing range.

Larramac and Grgat had, by this time, both recovered their senses and had their rifles at the ready. All four members of the assault party were aiming their weapons at the entrance of the cave even as they backed cautiously deeper into the interior.

Although she was sorry this confrontation had to happen at all, Dev was at least glad it had come about as it had. Had they been caught by the angels out in the open, the messengers of the gods would have had a much more deadly weapon available to them than lightning bolts. Though the angels were far smaller than a spaceship, their gravitic drive fields were still deadly at short range. They could have wafted silently down over the party and fried them all to death in seconds before the *Foxfire* group even knew what was happening. But the angels couldn't turn sideways and aim the drive fields into the cave, so they'd have to fight in a more honest fashion.

Another shape appeared at the entrance. Four beams lashed out simultaneously, though only three hit; Grgat was obviously frightened, and had forgotten most of the scanty training he'd had aboard *Foxfire*. The three hits were sufficient for a kill, though; this angel didn't even have time to unleash one of its lightning bolts before falling, mortally wounded, to the ground.

Dev, meanwhile, had been making some quick mental calculations. In the afterglow of the lasers and the lightning she was able to estimate the size of the cave opening and it was only three to three-and-a-half meters wide and high. The angels were close to four meters tall, and had a five-meter wing span when the wings were fully extended. She doubted the creatures would be able to come in here after them. If she and her crew could get out of direct line-of-sight of the cave mouth, they would probably be safe from the creatures' attack.

The angels must also have reached the same conclusion, for their battle tactics changed slightly. Because of the danger of their gravitic drive fields interacting, they could not work in close proximity to one another; but by remaining farther from the cave entrance, two of them could maintain their necessary separation and still both be in a straight line of sight to the interior.

This maneuver took them outside the effective range of the laser rifles, but it also left them at the very limit of their own range for lightning. The bolts came thick and fast, searing the air between them and the cave, but their accuracy suffered; the energy was spent harmlessly on the cave walls and floor.

Dev got awkwardly to her feet and moved back to where Dunnis was futilely firing his rifle at the distant angels. Turning off her radio so the robot Teddy Bears wouldn't hear her, she touched her helmet to his. "Use the cannon," she shouted.

In the heat of the battle, Dunnis had completely forgotten that he was carrying the personal energy cannon. He had been intent on the simplicity and quickness of the rifle, and had not given a thought to the more complex weapon strapped to his back. Dev helped him unpack it while their other two comrades continued their barrage of laser fire to keep the angels occupied.

Kneeling in the tunnel, Dev and Dunnis worked hastily to assemble the cannon. The base snapped together in three simple pieces, and the gun was placed easily in its cradle. Dunnis flipped up the range finder, took aim, and locked the co-ordinates into the gun's minicomputer. When the small green light appeared on the top of the barrel, he fired.

A ten-centimeter ball of pure energy rocketed out of the cannon's mouth, down the tunnel, and out into the night air. Like a bolide it left a blue-white trail of luminescence in its wake as it streaked with incredible speed toward its twin targets. Whether the angels saw it coming is a debatable point; even if they had noted its approach, they lacked the reflexes to react in time to save themselves.

The energy sphere struck the nearest angel just below its midsection. Instantly the sky outside was awash in brilliance as the power contained within the ball was released with explosive suddenness. The lower half of the angel was blown completely away and the upper half, totally powerless, tumbled out of the sky to the ground.

The angels had not suspected that the human party had weapons this efficient at its disposal. The second angel hovered in place, frozen by indecision. Before its creators could give it new orders, it was already doomed. Dunnis had reaimed his cannon and squeezed off a second shot.

This spheroid hit perfectly dead center. The whole planet seemed to shake with the impact, and the visual flash was eye-searing. Fragments of red-hot metal flew through the air in all directions, and when the humans could next look, the space outside their cave was totally empty.

Only six angels left, Dev thought. *They're bound to become more conservative now.*

Indeed, for a while it appeared that the gods' battle machines had become totally paralyzed. Whole minutes dragged by and, despite the vigilance of the four in the cave, nothing happened. The mouth of the tunnel remained dark and empty.

"What do you think they're up to?" Larramac asked.

"I don't know. It could be nearly anything." Dev shook her head to clear it of some of the fatigue. "But I wish they'd do something soon; I prefer honest fighting to just waiting around."

Within seconds she got her wish. The sky outside the cave mouth lit up with repeated flashes of the lightning, but none of the bolts came inside the tunnel. At the same time, the walls of the passageway were vibrating as though in a heavy earthquake. The shaking was strong enough to set Dev's teeth on edge.

"What are they doing?" Dunnis asked.

In answer, Dev could only point to the cave entrance. Against the background of repeated lightning flashes, they could see several small rocks shake loose from the ceiling of the cave and go crashing down the mountainside. As the bombardment continued larger rocks fell—and more frequently.

"Back!" Dev yelled. "They're trying to seal off the entrance."

They hurried further into the recesses of the cave, and just in time. A large section of the ceiling, weakened by the continual assault, fell to the floor with a crash that jarred them off their feet. More rubble fell on top of that, and even small pebbles from directly above them were shaken loose and rained down upon them.

After thirty seconds of chaos, the world became quiet once more. The entrance to their cave was completely

129

blocked with rubble. They were in total darkness, cut off from the outside world.

It was Dunnis who spoke first, his voice sounding tinny on Dev's radio as it came out of the utter blackness. "What do we do now?"

"I know what *I'm* doing," Dev said. "I'm getting out of this drumming suit."

Now that the direct threat from the angels was temporarily over, there was no need to maintain their suits' internal heat. Dev removed her helmet and breathed in a great chestful of air. The atmosphere within the tunnel was clogged with dust from the cave-in, but at least it was cool and didn't smell of her own overripe body. After a couple of deep breaths, she undid the fastening seam down the front of her spacer uniform and stepped out of it. The cool feeling of relief was immediate. It mattered not at all that she was now standing naked in a cave with two men and an alien; even if the tunnel had been lit with spotlights, the immodesty would have been a small price to pay for the comfort of cool air upon her skin.

Her idea seemed a popular one. Through the darkness she could hear the sounds of the other three undressing as well, stripping off both their uniforms and the by-now soggy padding that had been pressing against their bodies. The four of them luxuriated in the crisp air of the cavern, welcoming the chance to let their skin breathe. All other problems were forgotten in the pleasure of the moment.

It was, Dev estimated, about five minutes later that she decided their rest period was over for a while. They had to be brought back to the frightening reality. "All right, everyone put their suits back on. Don't bother with the padding—that trick won't work a second time, anyhow."

Without the extra stuffing inside their uniforms, they should be able to maintain comfortable temperatures; that was the way the suits were designed. "I'm going to put my helmet on, too, but not seal it. That way we can use the headlamps. No need to be so secretive in here; there's no one to spot us."

She waited a short while to make sure that everyone had had the chance to make themselves decent again, then switched on the light above her forehead. Again, after several minutes in the pitch blackness, the glare from the beam was blinding. Dev had to close her eyes and open them slowly to accustom them to the light. She had not had much chance to look around during their fight with the angels, and now seemed the best time to take stock. But what she saw as she glanced about startled her completely.

The floor beneath their feet was perfectly level except for some small rocks and miscellaneous debris jarred loose by the cave-in. The walls were straight and even, and the ceiling was a smooth arch over their heads. Behind them, the mass of rubble knocked loose by the angels blocked the entrance, while in front of them the passage continued on into the mountain for another twenty meters before disappearing into a darkness beyond the range of her lamp.

The four invaders stood silently observing this scene, letting the implications of what they saw filter slowly into their minds. Grgat in particular was gazing around awe-struck. This was a development none of them had expected.

"This at least solves one problem," Dev said at last.

"Eh?" Larramac and the others were startled out of their reveries by her statement, but the ship's owner recovered the quickest.

"I was afraid we'd be completely trapped in here, without food and with little water. We could probably dig our way out, but the angels would be waiting right on the other side of that rubble, and the instant we poked our heads out they'd blast us."

"We still may not be able to get out of here," Dunnis said gloomily.

"This is obviously an artificial corridor, and corridors have two ends," Dev pointed out. "Nobody builds a tunnel to nowhere."

"I'm worried about what we'll *find* at the other end," Larramac said.

"Ah, now that is indeed another question. I'm sure whatever it is will be on the side of the angels." Dev deliberately injected a note of false cheer into her voice. "But we've survived the nastiest things the gods have been able to throw at us so far; I have a feeling their arsenal might be running a trifle low."

"So is ours." Dunnis pointed behind them and Dev turned back toward the entrance. Their energy cannon, which they had abandoned rapidly when the roof began to cave in, lay smashed beneath a large piece of debris, totally useless.

Dev felt sickened by the cannon's loss. It had been their most potent armament. But she was determined to keep spirits up. "We're far from helpless, with our rifles, pistols, and grenade launchers. And the angels can't navigate in this tunnel, so we're safe on that score. I refuse to feel depressed until absolutely necessary."

She didn't even try to stifle the yawn that forced its way up from the depths of her body. "What I do feel is tired. I imagine you all feel the same."

They did, and they were also quite hungry. It had been twelve hours since they'd had any nourishment other than small sips of water. They had not packed any food along—they'd already been burdened with too much weight, in Dev's opinion—but they did have some nutrition pills. The pills would do nothing to ease the hunger gnawing at their stomachs, but at least they would keep up the group's energy levels.

"You all should get some rest before we go tramping down to the other end of this tunnel," Dev said. "I'll stand watch for a little while, then I'll wake someone to relieve me while I get a nap. We can't sleep for too long—the gods know where we are and I imagine they'll try something to destroy us—but we need some rest if we're going to be effective at all."

She did not have to tell them twice. The other three curled up instantly on the floor and were asleep almost before she'd finished speaking.

Dev sat down with her rifle in her lap and stared across at the smooth wall opposite her. Looking back on it, she was disappointed in herself that she'd been surprised by the tunnel's artificiality. The fact that she had discovered three of them was more than coincidental; there had to be a regular pattern to their placement along the mountainside. They must be access tunnels to the mountain's interior; it would make sense to position such corridors every so often up the slope if there were something inside the mountain worth getting to. Ideas were starting to form in her brain, and her lips twitched in a smile. Their fight might not be quite so hopeless, after all. The angels may even have done them a favor by cutting off the rest of their route up the mountain.

She suddenly became aware of a slight vibration in the floor. Sitting up straight, she listened and thought she detected a faint metallic clanking coming from the dark end of the tunnel. The sounds were just at the limit of her perception; it was hard to be positive she heard them at all. But in such a situation it could be fatal to wait for certainties.

Reaching out with her foot, she kicked lightly at the nearest sleeping figure. Larramac stirred and looked up at her groggily. "Time to get up already? I just got to sleep!"

"Shh," Dev whispered. "I think I hear something. Wake the others and tell them to get ready for a fight."

So saying, Dev turned off her light and stood up facing the far end of the corridor. If this was, as she suspected, a tunnel into the gods' private sanctuary, there was every reason to suspect an attack from that direction. The gods knew precisely where they were, and would not want them to remain here for any length of time.

Cautiously, while Larramac woke the others, Dev started down the corridor toward the unknown. She had her rifle and grenade launcher slung over her shoulders and her pistol ready in her hand. Her boots slid silently over the smooth floor, one slow, patient step at a time. She could not recall having ever been more frightened in her life, but she fought the emotion down. *Fear cripples*, she told herself. *It can change an ambiguous situation to a hopeless one. The fear lives in you, not in the event itself. Conquer the fear and you've won half the battle.*

It was easy advice to say, but harder to apply. Nevertheless, she continued walking forward.

Behind her she could hear the quiet stirrings of her comrades, but she tried to block out those sounds as much as possible. Ahead, those faint metallic scraping sounds were getting louder. She knew now that they were not just in her imagination—and they were getting closer all the time. Her hand tightened on the grip of her pistol.

Finally the noises grew so loud that Dev knew they were close. Distance was hard to estimate in this total darkness, but she doubted the makers of the noise were more than fifteen meters away. If she proceeded much further, she'd walk straight into them. She had been brave—or was that "foolhardy"?—to walk this far, but now she faced a decision. What should she make of this confrontation? With a determined click, she switched on her headlamp once more.

Standing before her was an army of robots. They varied in sizes and shapes—some were ovoid, others square; some were as big as three meters tall, others ranged in size down to only one meter. They were crowded closely together in the tunnel, and their ranks extended backward further than Dev could make out. It was impossible to make an accurate count of them; there could easily have been fifty or more jammed into the passageway. The first line was only seven meters away.

They had been moving slowly forward down the tunnel toward the group of invaders, but as the light came on suddenly they halted. Even robots could be startled by the unexpected, Dev mused. She herself stood still, momentarily blinded by the glare of her headlamp and the reflection of its beam off so many polished metallic surfaces. For a few breathless seconds the two sides stared at one another, unable to move.

Then the tableau was suddenly broken as the robots, abandoning their attempt to sneak up on the humans, surged forward at a faster pace. They were so crowded together that they could not move quickly without tripping over one another, but they did move with the relentless determination of machines that would do their designated job no matter what the obstacle.

Dev backpedaled quickly, knowing that if these robots shot at her she would make an easy target. But the robots did not fire; they merely marched forward after her. She gave them a closer inspection and noted, to her great surprise, that none of them seemed armed.

She brought up her own laser pistol and opened fire on one robot in the front ranks. Her shot hit true and burned a hole squarely through its brain case. The mechanical creature stumbled and fell forward, delaying the progress of those in line directly behind it. The rest of the front row continued their march, oblivious to the fate of their comrade, while the ones behind the fallen machine began stepping over it and kept coming.

Dev backed up a few more paces and fired again. Another robot fell, but still the line advanced upon her. *These robots don't need guns,* she realized. *They can crush us with their sheer numbers.*

From behind her she could hear running footsteps as her companions raced forward to her rescue. "They're not armed," she told them. "Just fire at will."

Laser beams lanced out of the darkness toward the gleaming metal army. One machine fell, then another, but the crowd behind them kept coming, scrambling over their brothers in their zombielike advance. The four invaders backed up a few more steps and tried again. Still more of the robots fell, and just as quickly others took their place.

"Let's hope they run out of robots before we run out of room," Dev said as she continued to fire into the oncoming ranks of machines.

"Let me go back and get my grenade launcher,"

Larramac said. "It could wipe a lot of them out at a single shot."

"No," Dev insisted. "Not in so confined an area. I don't want to risk another cave-in. Then we'd really be trapped. Let's try it the slow way for now."

The ranks of the robots were definitely thinning out. Their forward advance slowed as more and more of them fell beneath the laser fire of the humans. The ones in the rear took more time climbing over the scattered metal bodies on the floor before themselves becoming the victims of new laser beams.

The action quickly became a slaughter. After retreating halfway back to the site of the cave-in, the *Foxfire* party was able to hold its ground against any further withdrawal. Robots were dropping almost as fast as the crew could squeeze the firing buttons, but they continued to advance. At one point the invading quartet had to interrupt their shooting to change the power packs in their pistols, but it made little difference in the outcome of the battle. After half an hour, the floor of the cavern was littered with the motionless bodies of robots. In some places they were piled so high that it was next to impossible to climb past them.

Looking over the carnage, Dev could only shake her head sadly. "What a waste."

"Where did they all come from?" Dunnis asked.

"From inside the mountain," Dev replied. "I suspect these are the servants of the gods, just like the angels are their messengers. We're a lot closer to our goal than we would have guessed. The mountain is hollow and the gods live inside it, not on top of it."

"You mean . . . all of this is artificial?" Larramac waved a hand and looked around him in amazement. The concept of a mountain this huge being totally manufactured was frightening.

Dev nodded. "That's my guess, at least. Do you remember my telling you the gods would need an enormous computer facility to correlate all the data they receive from their bugs? That's what Mount Orrork is—one vast computer complex. Those robots of various sizes and shapes are probably part of the maintenance team—a place this large needs a lot of upkeep.

"That would also explain why they were unarmed. Maintenance robots wouldn't have guns, whereas soldier robots would. And that means . . ."

She paused and looked into each of their faces. "And that means we've managed to penetrate inside their defenses. They aren't equipped to fight inside their stronghold; all their weapons—the big guns and the angels—are for defending the outside of their fortress. They won't work inside. Barring a few surprises they may still have up their sleeves, our opposition will definitely be less formidable from this point on."

Dev felt a thrill inside her as she spoke those words. The gods had taken their best shots, and yet the *Foxfire* party was unscathed. Now was the time to fight back. From now on it was her group that would be attacking and the gods on the defensive.

11

"There is nothing common about common sense."
—Anthropos, *The Godhood of Man*

There were smiles on the faces of the other three. While it was good that they were feeling more confident, a little of that spirit could go a long way.

"That doesn't mean it's going to be easy," Dev continued. "We can't afford to get careless at this stage of the game. They probably still have a lot of robots left, and one of those big ones could crush any of us to a pulp."

"But you're right," Larramac said, smiling. "We've got them on the run now, and we have to take the offensive immediately or lose our advantage." All feeling of hunger or fatigue had vanished from his body. He was now gripped with the same power-lust that had started them on this venture in the first place.

Dev sighed. The others had all managed to catch at least a few minutes of sleep in the tunnel before the robot attack. She'd had none. Larramac was right, though—their time was now, and they dared not lose the initiative. It was her job to lead the assault no matter how tired she was.

Responsibility may be the key to sanity, Dev thought, *but it sure plays havoc with your sleep pattern.*

"All right," she said. "But there are still some precautions we'll have to take. We'll go in with our suits sealed up."

"Why?" Larramac demanded. "If that mountain is their personal stronghold, there'll be air in there. The gods have to breathe too, don't they?"

"Probably—but robots don't. They could attempt to seal off the area we're in and either evacuate the atmosphere or else pump in some poisonous gas. In either case, our helmets are a simple enough precaution against that, don't you agree?"

The ship's owner did admit Dev had a point. They returned to their campsite and packed up the rest of their belongings, then walked warily down the tunnel into the mountain.

"These caves were probably access routes while the mountain was being built," Dev surmised as they walked. "Access tunnels are necessary for a variety of reasons. Once the mountain was completed, the tunnels were left as emergency routes. The gods never figured anyone could invade them this way—all their defenses are oriented toward keeping people as far from here as possible."

When they came to the site of their successful battle they had to proceed much more slowly, climbing over the bodies of the fallen robots that littered the floor. In several spots they had to proceed one at a time, as there was barely room for a single individual to crawl through the open space. Once past the battleground, they made much better progress and came, quite abruptly, to the end of the tunnel.

The arched doorway before them left little doubt that this was an entrance to some more official place within the mountain, but at present a thick slab of metal blocked further movement. Dev went up and pressed against it, but it wouldn't budge. Running her hands over its surface, she could feel no seams; apparently it was one large piece of metal that came down from the ceiling to the tunnel's floor and barred their path to the interior.

"They've sealed us off," Dev stated the obvious. "If they can't kill us with their robots, at least they can try to keep us out of their domain. Even the four of us together couldn't lift that slab."

"Stand back," Dunnis said. "I'll see if I can burn a way through."

Dev and the others obediently stepped behind the engineer as the big man took his laser rifle off his shoulder and concentrated its energy point blank at the center of the slab. The area under fire heated up, first red hot and then progressing to white as Dunnis continued to direct his beam at it. But after three solid minutes he still had nothing to show for his efforts but a pinhole that went about a centimeter deep into the metal.

"Looks like we'll need another tactic," Dev said softly. She'd known Dunnis's attempt would fail—that door was entirely too thick and heavy—but had seen no point to telling him that in advance. It was better that he should feel useful.

"Yes, probably the grenade launchers would be a better tool here," Larramac said.

Dev shook her head. "Even a grenade or two probably wouldn't have the necessary impact to blast through that door."

"Then what do you suggest?"

She turned to Dunnis. "Have you got the spare energy cartridge for the cannon?"

"I think so." The engineer searched through his pockets and pulled out the white plastic cartridge. Dev took it from him and examined it. It was hard to believe that a little box only ten centimeters by five by three could hold such a fantastic amount of energy.

"I don't know if this will work," Dev admitted as she placed the cartridge on the ground beside the middle portion of the door. "But if it does work, it'll be pretty spectacular. We'd better all get as far from here as possible." She started walking back down the corridor; the others joined her.

Dev and her group took up a position behind the barricade of robot bodies. From this distance, the cartridge was barely visible as a small white spot at the limits of their headlamps' glow. "Now to test my marksmanship," she muttered.

Taking her rifle off her shoulder once more, Dev propped it securely on one of the motionless robots and sighted through the range finder. Holding her aim as steady as she could, she squeezed the trigger. The laser beam at first was slightly high and to the left of her target; with clinical precision she adjusted it until the ruby beam was hitting the cartridge dead center.

For almost half a minute nothing happened. Dev had not been expecting instant reaction; the manufacturers of those cartridges made them tough. The energy stored in that small plastic container was the equivalent of several tons of chemical explosive. It had to be rigidly safeguarded against accidental release.

But in the continual discharge of laser energy for thirty seconds was more than the contents could be protected from. Without any warning at all, the cartridge exploded, releasing all its energy in one tremendous blast.

One second the corridor was deathly quiet, the only sound being the faint humming of Dev's rifle; the next, there was a roar that threatened to deafen them all. The concussion knocked them sprawling over backward even though they were more than twenty meters away. The pile of robots came toppling down upon them, tangling them in a mass of mechanical limbs and bodies. The ground shook beneath them and rocks from the ceiling rained down, pelting them mercilessly.

Dunnis's voice reached Dev's ears over the radio, even though she couldn't see him as he was buried under some robots beneath her. "You sure don't believe in halfway measures, do you, Captain?"

"Whatever it takes to get the job done."

She shook her head to clear it and bring her eyes back into focus once more. She was lying on her back, enmeshed in the parts of several robots, looking up at the ceiling. The rock overhead was seriously cracked, and looked as though it might give way any second. She struggled to a sitting position and looked down the corridor to the door, but she couldn't see that far—the intervening space was clogged with dust jarred loose by the blast. There was no way of knowing whether her trick had worked—but if that hadn't managed to knock a hole in the door, there was nothing else at their disposal that would work any better.

She rose shakily to her feet and climbed off the junk heap, then reached in to give her companions a hand extricating themselves. It took a few minutes, but eventually they were all standing in the passageway, stunned but otherwise unharmed. All their equipment was intact, so Dev began leading them back toward the door.

They had barely gone ten meters when the roof collapsed over their former position, burying the robot corpses under a pile of rubble. The four looked back silently and shivered.

Dev broke the silence. "Well, we can't go back that way again." *As if we ever could.* "Let's press on and hope they heard our knock."

When they were five meters away, they saw that the blast had indeed been successful. There was a gaping hole where once there had been the solid slab of metal. Rays of light shone through into the tunnel from the region beyond. Not only the slab, but most of the wall as well had been blown away, leaving a hole nearly four meters across for them to pick their way through.

They crossed the portal cautiously, taking care not to touch the jagged edges around them, which were still red hot in some cases. On the other side of the doorway, they found more robot bodies, mangled this time almost out of all recognition.

"They must have been waiting here to ambush us in case we found some way of opening the door," Dev surmised. "They weren't expecting such a violent entry."

There had been major damage caused on this side of the wall as well. Tall banks of instruments reached right to the ceiling a full five meters above their heads, but some of the nearer banks had had large chunks torn out of them by pieces of flying debris. Aisles a meter and a half wide separated each row of banks, but the nearer ones were strewn with rubble. The place was deathly quiet, and there was no sign of movement. The invaders could have been alone inside the mountain for all they could tell.

On looking around, it became obvious that this was the computer complex Dev had imagined. Though the setup had been designed and built by aliens, form followed function—and the three humans had been in too many computer facilities not to recognize it for what it was.

"Imagine a whole mountain like this," Dunnis whispered, awed by the scale of the works around him.

"Yes," Larramac said, "but the place looks deserted. Where is everybody?"

"Most of the servants stationed at this level probably met us in the tunnel," Dev said. "The rest were standing guard inside the door when we blew it open. At the moment there probably isn't anyone else on this floor. My guess, though, is that the gods will redirect some personnel here on the double. I'd suggest we keep moving if we don't want to be trapped."

To set the example, she started off down a row that extended immediately ahead of them. Silent computer banks towered up on either side of her, cold and mysterious, and the aisle extended so far before her that perspective shrank the other end to a dot. There was no particular reason why she chose this direction over any other; she just felt the need to be moving, and any direction would serve until she knew a little more about which way she was going.

The others followed slowly after her, gawking and craning their necks to either side as though they were walking through a medieval cathedral. "Don't you think it's a little unusual," Larramac remarked, "that so far we haven't seen a single living creature? There are the angels, the robots, this computer—but where are the gods themselves?"

"I don't have the answer for that one yet, but I have the definite feeling we'll both find out at the same time."

"You know what? I'm beginning to think there aren't any gods. Maybe this whole setup was established to run automatically and the gods died off somewhere along the way, yet the whole crazy scheme continues along of its own momentum."

"It's certainly possible," Dev conceded. She was pleased that her boss was actually doing some serious thinking for a change. "Or, if they're not nonexistent, they at least are very few in number. They've lived in this mountain for what appears to be centuries at the least, possibly even millennia. If they weren't capable of breeding, they'd certainly have died off by now. If they did breed, they'd have to keep their numbers very limited or they'd overrun this sanctuary of theirs. What we're fighting—what we've always been fighting— is essentially a small force with very great resources."

"One advantage we have," Dunnis chimed in, "is that they can hardly launch a major attack against us in here. If they tried any fireworks, they'd be damaging their own computer equipment. They wouldn't risk that, would they?"

Dev was quite pleasantly surprised. Even her inert engineer was making shrewd observations. *Proximity to these computers must have salutary effects,* she thought. *Maybe thinking is contagious.* "Probably not."

"But we *can* risk it," Larramac said. "I'll bet we could lob a few grenades into these computer banks and really drum up their operations." There was a feral gleam in his eye that Dev didn't like at all.

"No!" she answered firmly. Wanton destruction violated her sense of aesthetics and ethics, but she knew she'd have to come up with more concrete reasons than that if she were to dissuade her boss from wreaking havoc throughout this complex. "For one thing, we don't know what's controlled by these particular portions of the computer. Blowing them up might result in one of the angels blasting an entire village out of existence. Or the whole mountain might blow sky high, with us inside it.

"Besides, we're only immune to attack up to a certain point. As long as we don't do any terrible damage they may leave us alone for a while. But if our destruction gets too far out of hand . . . well, just ask any doctor. He'd rather amputate a limb than risk the health of the entire body. If we become too severe an 'infection,' the gods may decide amputation is the best alternative— and they probably have the power to do that. I'd rather let them think they can contain us here until the last possible moment."

Of course, no metaphor was totally accurate. Ampu-

144

tation was not always possible if the infection were in the torso or head—but Dev had no idea where such vital areas within this computer complex were.

Larramac accepted her argument, but he made it clear he didn't like it. The overeager boy within him would have loved nothing better than to run around leaving rampant destruction in his wake. Dev realized she'd been lucky so far, but how much longer would she be able to keep those rash impulses of his in check?

The aisle in which they were traveling was criss-crossed every ten or so meters by a perpendicular path, establishing the floor pattern as a rectangular grid. They had crossed seven intersections already and the far end of the aisle appeared no nearer than it had when they began. As they crossed the eighth intersection, however, Dev caught a brief glimpse of movement off to the side. By the time she could turn her head to look it had vanished, but she knew there had been *something* there.

"This way!" she shouted, heading down the corridor where the movement had been. "I saw somebody go by down here."

The others were on her heels as she raced along the pathway. Several rows down, she saw a robot running full speed along one bank of instruments. Thinking it might lead them somewhere significant—and not having any better direction to travel in herself—she followed after it.

They were halfway down one row when two things happened simultaneously. The lights throughout this level of the mountain went out, leaving them in darkness as complete as that in the cave. This in itself would not have been too great a handicap, since they did have the headlamps on their helmets. However, at the same time as their world went dark, the walls started falling in on them.

It had been an ambush, Dev realized belatedly, a trick to get them running down this particular aisle. This section of the computer was probably not as vital as others, and the gods were willing to sacrifice it in order to wipe out the alien invaders.

Several robots waiting in the next row over must have been pushing hard against one computer bank and, in the dark, it fell over onto the raiding party. If the sheer bulk had been able to hit the four intruders completely it would have squashed them flat into the floor, but fortunately the gods had, in their rush (or was it panic?), overlooked the basic geometry of the situation.

Each stack of the equipment reached to the ceiling, which was five meters high, while the aisles between banks were only a meter and a half wide. As the towering wall fell over, it hit the next wall before it could crush the people in the aisle. The force of its impact caused that bank, in turn, to topple over, and a domino effect began to build. All along the chain, computer banks fell to the ground, knocking over the next in turn. The floor resounded with a continual crashing sound that almost rivaled the explosion of the energy cartridge in volume. The sound had almost died out when the echo reached them. The closed level caused noise to reverberate inside it, rattling them all to the core. It was more than two minutes before the sound began to die away.

The *Foxfire* party was knocked to the ground, but not crushed. One end of the wall that had fallen on them now rested on the bottom of the wall it had knocked over, thus leaving a wedge-shaped gap through which the invaders could still move. "I think they lost on that idea," Dev said quietly when the noise stopped. "But it was an awfully close call. We'd better get out of here and moving again before they think of anything better."

Taking the lead once more, Dev crawled to the next intersection and looked around. She knew there were robots around; after all, someone had knocked that wall over onto them. But none were immediately visible to her in the darkness. She switched on her headlamp and then, gun in hand, she pulled herself out of the mess and stood up in the intersection.

Dunnis had crawled out behind her and was starting to get to his feet when Dev spotted the monster. It reached almost to the ceiling, a cylinder with heavy legs bearing down on her. Its arms were puny in comparison to its body, but the arms were not what Dev was worried about. A robot that size could easily mass six or seven hundred kilograms, and that was nothing she wanted to tangle with.

Instinctively she fired up at it. Her laser beam sliced through it as easily as it had gone through the others, but with a behemoth this large it was harder to hit a crucial area. The legs pounded on, covering the intervening distance at an alarming rate. Dev shot several more times through different portions of its body, trying desperately to stop its advance.

At last one of her beams hit something vital. The creature came to a halt with one foot extended, wavered back and forth for a moment, then began to fall directly toward her. Even "dead" it could still kill her if any of its incredible bulk landed squarely.

Dev pushed the startled Dunnis backward, onto the top of the wall he'd just climbed out from under. Using the reaction from that effort, she leaped forward into the next aisle. The robot hit ground with a thunderous crash right at the spot the two humans had vacated just seconds before.

Feeling like the biblical David, Dev stood up and brushed herself off, then turned around to look at the Goliath she had slain. She hoped there were not too many more creatures of that size lying in wait for them throughout the mountain.

"All right, the coast seems clear for the moment," she said. "Everyone out of hiding. We have to get moving again."

Dunnis rose unsteadily to his feet once more while Grgat and Larramac climbed out from under the fallen wall. Dev started walking forward again, becoming more impatient with every step. The inside of this mountain was a big place; they might roam around for days and not find where the gods were hiding. So far they had discovered no significant clues, and she was becoming a little upset with herself.

A clanking sound reached them from further along in the mountain. They'd heard that sound before—an advancing army of robots. Only this time they were making no attempt to be silent and sneak up on the invaders. This, now, was all out war.

It was hard to tell precisely where the sound was originating, and their headlamps did not penetrate the darkness far enough for them to see the army yet. All they could do was keep walking forward, rifles at the ready, until they spotted the enemy.

After they'd gone another fifty meters the robot horde came into sight. This was a group to make the first batch look trivial. They must easily have numbered in the hundreds, and they were all marching toward the *Foxfire* party with a single determined purpose—to crush these intruders into the ground.

"I think," Dev said calmly, "now is the time for the grenade launchers."

She strapped her rifle back around her shoulder as she spoke and pulled out the grenade launcher she'd been carrying all this time. The weapon was short and stubby, looking very much like a sawed-off shotgun with a single large barrel. The grenades it fired were contained in a clip in the stock, and were just over eight centimeters in diameter. Each clip held five grenades.

The robots were moving with surprising speed. By the time Dev had gotten her launcher out and ready, the machines had closed the distance to within fifty meters. If they got much closer Dev wouldn't dare fire the grenades, or the explosion would affect her own party as well.

She had no time to aim. Bringing the launcher up quickly, she fired straight ahead into the onrushing crowd of robots. The grenade landed in the middle of the forward line and exploded on impact. The force of the blast tore ten robots apart directly and scattered large pieces of them into some of their compatriots, disabling them as well.

Dev, however, did not wait to see the success of her first shot; instead, she lobbed a second shot over the heads of the first group and into a congested middle bunch of the machines. The second explosion was even more successful, destroying a score of the robots.

Beside her, Larramac was using his grenade launcher in a more deliberate but equally effective manner. He was taking advantage of the fact that the robots were forced to travel through the comparatively narrow aisles between the computer banks as they attacked, and placing his shots in the middle of crowded aisles. Each grenade destroyed between twenty and thirty of the foe, yet they came relentlessly on.

Dunnis and Grgat were keeping busy as well, using their laser rifles to dispatch more of the enemy. The rifles were slower and less efficient, but the robots made easy targets. Packed as close together as they were, it was nearly impossible not to hit *something* with a beam fired straight ahead.

And yet, despite all the havoc they were wreaking, Dev got the distinct impression her side was losing. Already more than a hundred robots had been destroyed, yet there were hundreds more behind them, ready to carry on the battle. She and Larramac only had a few more spare clips for their grenade launchers, and she shuddered to think what would happen when that ammunition ran out.

"We'll have to run for it," she shouted, even though the radio would carry her words to her friends' ears no matter what the volume of her voice.

"Why?" Larramac asked. "We're holding them off all right."

"If these were living soldiers they'd have a fear of death—we could hope to frighten them into giving up the attack and running away. But nothing is going to stop those robots. There's still more of them than we can handle—unless you think there's something particularly holy about dying on this spot." She began running down the cross corridor to her left and the others, reluctantly, followed.

"What are you trying to do?" Larramac gasped as he ran.

"Outflank them. We're faster and more maneuverable

than they are. If we can get around behind them, we may have a chance."

"How do you figure?" Dunnis puffed. "They can turn around and be just as dangerous from the back as from the front."

Grgat was not able to keep up with them. The tight boots were torturing his broad, flat feet. He had been limping before, but now his lopsided gallop would have been comical if the situation were not so serious. Glancing over her shoulder, Dev saw that he was already lagging ten meters behind the rest and falling further back each second.

Coming to a halt herself, Dev waited for the other two men to pass her and went back to look after the Daschamese. "Are you all right?" she asked.

The native had not spoken much since their assault had begun hours ago. He was gasping now as he said, "I have caused you nothing but trouble. Go on without me now. You'll stand a better chance."

That may well have been true, but Dev still had a few principles to which she adhered rigidly—and not abandoning a friend was one of them. "Nonsense, we'll be okay. Gros, Roscil, come back here. Grgat can put his arms around your shoulders and you can support him."

Larramac turned to face her, open revolt in his eyes. "We can't let him drag us down with him," he said. "If he can't keep up, let him stay behind. We all knew the risks when we started out."

It was all Dev could do to hold her temper in restraint. They had no time for a shouting match. "In case you've forgotten," she said through nearly clenched teeth, "we need Grgat to be our liaison to the rest of Dascham once we've eliminated the gods. He was the one who promised you the reward, remember?"

The expression of rebellion wavered on Larramac's face. *His problem,* Dev decided, *is that he has no principles to give him a steady direction.* "Come on, quickly," she continued with all the power she could squeeze into her voice. "We still have a chance if you hurry."

Dunnis came back to obey and Larramac, after a

long moment's hesitation, did the same. There was a look of hatred for Dev in his eyes, though; he did not like to be beaten in public. He was storing up grudges against her, of that she was sure; she only hoped he wouldn't try to collect the payment before this fiasco was over.

With the two men supporting Grgat's weight, they started off again, moving as quickly as they could. Dev was pleasantly surprised to find that even carrying the native as they were, they were still capable of moving at about three quarters of their unencumbered speed. The process might take a little longer, but they still had a chance to outflank the robots.

"You still haven't answered my question," Dunnis panted as they ran. "Why are we trying to get behind them?"

"All those robots weren't on this floor to begin with," Dev explained. "They had to come here from other floors. And to do that, they needed a gravtube or something similar. Going back in the direction they came from is the best way to locate it—and we need a gravtube if we're going to find the gods, because it's not likely they're on this level."

That explanation seemed to satisfy her companions, and they proceeded for a time in silence. The robots had become aware of their change in direction; Dev kept track of their progress every time she crossed an intersection. The entire mechanical horde had turned to the side and was still pursuing them, getting closer all the time. There was no sign yet of thinning in their ranks that would indicate the *Foxfire* party was reaching the rear of their formation.

Occasionally Dev would stop for a moment, let her companions go by, and lob a grenade into the midst of the oncoming robots. The explosions produced a satisfactory amount of damage, but hardly seemed to slow the enemy's advance at all. Frustrated, she would continue on.

Finally, though, the numbers of robots on their right became less, indicating the bulk of the army was now behind them. "This way now," Dev called, moving down one cross path to her right. The others followed, but ever more slowly. It was clear Dunnis and Larramac were tiring from carrying Grgat's weight all this while. Dev hoped they would not have much further to go before finding the tube she wanted.

The robots had reversed themselves and were coming after them again. Dev knew they might have to stand and fight once more, but she didn't want to. Ideally, what she wanted to do was to find that tube and leave this level before the robots could reach them.

After running a zigzag pattern through the aisles of computer banks for another three minutes, it was Dunnis who spotted the tube first. "There," he cried, and the others moved instinctively the way he pointed.

Dev had never seen an elevator shaft this large in all her life—though considering the vast numbers of robots it could carry she should not have been surprised. The tube was a long cylinder almost twenty meters in diameter; it extended up and down further than she could see. There were other differences between it and the gravtubes that were standard on human worlds—subtle ones, but enough to give her doubts about the way the tube operated.

Taking out her grenade launcher again, she fired a grenade down the shaft. It seemed to take forever before they heard the explosion, very far away. They could see tiny sparks flying and crackling; Dev's shot had had the desired effect.

Larramac put Grgat down and shook his captain by her shoulders. "What did you do that for?"

"I had to put the tube out of commission. For one thing, it keeps them from transferring any more robots from level to level. For another, it keeps them from presenting us with any nasty surprises—like turning on the power once we're inside the shaft . . . or turning it off and letting us fall."

"But how do we use it now?"

Dev flashed her light to indicate the series of rungs along the wall of the shaft near the opening. "Manually," she said. "We climb down, the same as we climbed up the mountain."

"Down?" Larramac was puzzled. "But the gods live on top of Orrork."

"Grgat never said that," Dev snapped. They didn't have much time before the robot army arrived, and she was becoming impatient with her boss's stupidity. "We are basing our assumption on the old Earth myths of Olympus and such. But think for a second. You're part of a small contingent, losers in a space war. You come here, and you're extremely defense-oriented. You build an entire mountain to serve as your headquarters. Where are you going to live? Right at the top, the most exposed position possible? Or down at the absolute bottom, with tons of equipment interposed between you and any possible enemy? My money's on finding them in the basement."

Larramac looked as though he wanted time to consider Dev's argument. But there was no time. Already, the clanking sounds of the advancing robots were coming ominously closer. "You can stand there if you want," Dev told him, "but as for me, I'm going down right now."

Reaching inside for the nearest rung, she swung herself into the shaft and began her descent.

12

"Guilt is a tempting trap for the unwary. It lets you feign responsibility while wallowing in ego."
— Anthropos, *The Sane Mind*

It didn't take long for the other three to decide she was right. Barely had she begun to climb down the rungs when she noticed Grgat and Dunnis coming just above her, the native limping noticeably. Larramac, after but a moment's hesitation, joined them. They were now in the final part of their assault, and Dev kept all her weary senses alert for signs of trouble.

The rungs that projected out from the wall of the elevator shaft were semicircular tubes of metal about thirty centimeters across, but were spaced oddly apart for the humans. Built originally to accommodate robots and/or the gods as an emergency route, they were closer together than was considered standard in human society. Dev found that she either had to take shorter steps or longer ones, and either way affected her pace. She finally decided to make many of the shorter steps, although doing so meant more frequent use of her already overabused muscles.

The shaft was as dark as the mountainside had been during their earlier climb. Dev descended as rapidly as the short steps allowed, worried that the gods would try some new tricks while the invaders were in such a comparatively helpless position. The thought crossed her mind that she might suddenly step off one rung and into empty space, falling to her death hundreds of meters below, but she dismissed that fear as too ridiculous. These rungs had been set at regular intervals in this wall for emergency use by the gods should the need arise. They would hardly go to the trouble of tricking themselves.

She thought she detected a sudden motion close by, but when she turned her head the flashlight beam revealed nothing but empty air. A moment later, however, she distinctly felt something brush by the edge of her suit on its way downward to the floor. "Did somebody drop something?" she asked.

"It's the robots," said Larramac, who was highest on the ladder and could see what was going on at the level they'd just left. "They're throwing things down at us from the doorway. Not heavy things, apparently, just whatever comes to hand."

"They don't have to be heavy," Dev said. "They've got gravity working on their side."

Privately she was cursing herself out for all sorts of a fool for failing to anticipate this problem. Bombardment was the simplest and most effective weapon the robots would have in this situation. Gravitational acceleration on Dascham was approximately equal to that on Earth, meaning that a falling object gained speed at the rate of ten meters per second per second. Initial mass was scarcely a factor; even a marble could be deadly if it fell from a great enough height.

This bombardment would only get more and more hazardous the lower they went. And they would have to move quickly the instant they reached bottom, for fear that the robots would toss a pile of stuff down on top of them and crush them against the floor.

"We'd better slow our pace a little," she said. "Hug as close to the wall as you possibly can and make sure of every step. The only thing in our favor is that it'll be harder for them to aim the further away from them we are."

Listening to her own advice, she hunched her body up tightly against the side of the shaft. More debris flashed by her in ever-increasing amounts. She caught sight of some of it in the beam of her headlamp. These weren't marbles the robots were throwing, but machine parts. Either they had gone back and scavenged pieces of their comrades who had fallen in the chase or else they were deliberately dismantling themselves in the effort to stop the invaders.

Roscil will have it worst, she thought. *He's right at the top of the line, the first target. I have three other bodies ahead of me; I should be relatively protected.*

Unfortunately it didn't work that way.

A large piece of metal hit her hard on the right shoulder just at the instant she had taken her left hand off a rung to switch to a lower one. The blow was a glancing one, not extremely painful, but it startled her enough to make her let go of her hold with her right hand as well. She realized the mistake the instant she made it, and flailed out with her arms to try to catch something. The fingers of her left hand brushed a rung but could not grasp it. With an involuntary shriek she fell over backward into the darkness.

There was a sharp snapping sensation and a pain shot up the length of her left leg. She gasped and cried out a second time. The world seemed funny and her head was spinning, but the fall had stopped. Her left leg felt on fire. She tried to tilt her head upward to see what the situation was.

As she fell, her left foot had slipped through the metal loop of the rung it was on, and had lodged there, saving her life. She was now hanging upside down in the darkened shaft, suspended by that one leg. The pain was throbbing; her left ankle was at least sprained if not actually broken. But that was preferable to her entire body lying shattered on the bottom of the shaft this moment.

Between harsh pants she told her companions what had happened, and to be careful not to climb down onto her foot as they descended. Grgat was next in line above her and, as he came down, he shone his light on her body.

"I will try to reach you," he said. Standing on the rung just above the one where her foot was caught, the native kept hold of the wall with one hand and tried to reach out for her with his other. Dev strained against gravity to reach upward toward him, but was afraid to try too hard; she didn't want her foothold to loosen and send her plunging down to the ground.

But the alien was simply too short; there was no way he could reach the captain's outstretched hand.

"Wait a minute," Dev panted. "I've got an idea." The rope they had used for climbing up the mountainside was still tied around her waist. Unfastening one end of it, she flung it at the native. "Catch this."

Her throw was very bad and didn't even come close to him on the first few tries. It kept falling back into her face, and she doubted she'd ever get it right. The pain in her foot was so severe she could hardly see straight any more, and she could feel the grip weakening. Blood was rushing to her head; her temples were pounding. If she didn't make it soon, she knew, she'd lose out completely and slip away to a quick death.

The next throw was a success. Grgat was able to catch onto the line and pull it tight. Dev closed her eyes thankfully and began pulling herself up. Her arms felt like rubber as she strained. More debris than ever was now sailing past her, and she had a vivid image of being struck by another piece and knocked completely loose just as rescue was within her grasp.

The muscles at her waist were tight and sore as she strained them to lean forward. Grgat had one hand holding tightly to a rung while the other hand was reaching out, holding the rope securely. When Dev had pulled herself up high enough she stretched one hand toward the wall and managed to catch hold of the rung just above the one on which Grgat was standing. "Made it," she gasped, so that the two men above would know she was safe.

A large, heavy piece of metal came sailing down the shaft. From what Dev could see, it was irregular in shape, part of a piece of machinery. Grgat was still leaning outward, not having had the chance yet to pull himself back against the wall. The piece of metal struck him squarely and hard on the back of his helmet.

Space helmets were built to withstand as much abuse as the designers could imagine, including meteroid impact. Grgat's helmet did not shatter from the blow, though the sound of the contact resounded through this portion of the elevator shaft. Coming as unexpectedly as it did, however, the hit stunned the Daschamese. His head tilted sharply forward and his hands released their grip on the rungs. He fell past Dev into the abyss.

Dev had only just regained her own hold when her source of support was knocked away, and instinctively, she reached out with her other hand to grab another rung and steady herself. She had no hands left with which to reach for Grgat's falling form. And so he fell, while all she could do was watch him drop out of her sight to his death on the floor of the shaft below them.

She gripped the rungs tightly and found her hands shaking. Grgat had just saved her life, and she'd been unable to return the favor. Her own close call had put her in a mild state of shock; the death of one of her companions sent her even deeper. Pulling herself close against the wall, she held the rungs in a frantically tight grip and began sobbing openly.

It's my responsibility, she thought over and over. *I failed him. I should have been able to do something.* The rest of the Universe seemed to vanish, and she was alone with herself.

"Captain?" A soft voice intruded in her void. She recognized it as Dunnis's, but she was too deep in her own shock to react.

"Captain, I know you feel sorry about him, but we can't stand here forever."

Why not? Dev wondered. This whole raid had been a fiasco from the start. They'd never had a chance against the superior forces arrayed against them. Why shouldn't they simply stand here forever and die like the insignificant specks they were? Her sobbing continued unabated.

"Dev, snap out of this!" Larramac's voice cut through the fog of her mind. "Don't go soft and feminine on me now—we've got to keep moving!"

Soft and feminine? In spite of herself, Dev felt all the old insults, all the old abuses rising to the surface. The snickering of the crews on past ships she'd commanded, the unuttered thought in the minds of prospective employers: *She can't be a good captain, she's a woman. She won't be able to take the pressure.*

She drumming well would keep moving. They couldn't be allowed to see her like this.

She tested her left foot and was rewarded with a bolt of fire racing up the entire leg. This would make things more difficult. Holding tightly to the rungs with both hands, she lowered her right foot gingerly to the next lower rung. Then, with great care, she moved one hand at a time downward to grab the next. It was not the fast gait she'd maintained before her accident, but it would get her where she was going.

Above her, the two men saw her start moving once more and she could hear their sighs of relief. The expedition was on the march again.

Dev tried to clear her mind and concentrate solely on her climbing, which was difficult enough. Thoughts, however, kept intruding. She replayed in her memory the scene of the piece of metal striking Grgat's helmet. The way his head had snapped forward, the impact of the blow may have snapped his neck, which would make her inability to catch him totally superfluous. He might have been dead before letting go of the ladder— and that would account for the fact that he didn't cry out as he fell.

He wanted to come along, Dev reminded herself sternly. *He knew the odds were vastly against us—we all did. But he came.*

Looked at in a coldly logical light, they shouldn't even have made it this far. Her own expectations had never been this high; she'd been prepared to die on the slopes outside, victim of a quick lightning blast. For all four of them to survive to the elevator shaft was nothing short of miraculous. Instead of feeling guilty that one of their number had died, she should be proud that her tactics against an overwhelming enemy had resulted in only 25 per cent losses after this long.

"Guilt is a tempting trap," she quoted as she continued her labored descent down the tube. It was also, she knew, a debilitating, paralyzing one.

The rain of junk had become a downpour. Sometimes even a whole robot would be flung at them. All of them were being hit now occasionally by a piece of debris, but they were taking greater care not to let go of their handholds. All three were in pain from numerous bruises, and the muscles in their bodies complained as they climbed further downward for what seemed like kilometers.

Reaching down for the next rung, Dev's foot hit instead a loose piece of metal. The accumulation of debris had completely covered the floor of the shaft. Dev was afraid to look around for a moment, afraid that the sight of Grgat's smashed body would be more than she could take. But the heap of junk was so deep by this time it had completely buried the native. There was only the irregular footing, plus the constant bombardment of new debris.

There was no opening outward to the mountain's bottom level, which worried Dev at first—what if the debris had piled so high that it completely blocked the doorway? But that fear vanished instantly. This shaft was twenty meters in diameter; filling it to a depth of more than a meter or two would take a good proportion of all the robots they had seen on the upper level—and surely not that much junk had rained down on them yet.

Now that they were at the very bottom, though, they were at the most dangerous position. All the robots at the top would have to do was toss a large enough pile of scrap down at them and they could hardly miss. Their only hope was that the robots wouldn't know they had made it all the way down yet.

In an attempt to keep it that way, Dev turned off her radio and waited beside the ladder as the other two men came down. One at a time, she touched their helmets with her own, alerting them to communicate in this manner until they were out of danger, and to hug the wall as tightly as they could. Also, they would have to turn out their headlamps and work in the dark once more; if the robots above saw the lights moving around, they would know the trio had reached bottom.

With the lights out, Dev felt her way cautiously around the rim of the circular shaft. She reasoned that the door would be within a couple of meters, at most, of the ladder, in roughly the same relative position it had been on the upper level. As she'd guessed, her fingers could feel the break in the otherwise smooth walls that indicated the presence of a currently-closed doorway. The problem now would be getting it open.

She decided to confer with the others in a three-way helmet-touching conference. "We can't really force the door open by pushing it or sliding it. The only alternative I can see is blowing it open, like we did to the cave door. As soon as we do that, though, it'll alert the robots upstairs that we've made it down here, and they'll drop everything they've got on us. We'll have to shoot a grenade at the door and then rush through before whatever the robots drop can reach us."

"How long will the load take to fall?" Larramac asked.

"Good question. How far down do you think we climbed? I'd estimate about a quarter of a kilometer."

"It felt like at least ten kilometers," Dunnis said. "But I think you're probably right."

Dev stuck that figure into the simple equation for time as a function of distance and gravitational acceleration. She was hampered by the difficulty of doing the square root in her head, and wished her pocket computer were more accessible, "Very roughly, I'd say we had about seven seconds. It might be a little more, depending on how quick their reflexes are once they hear the blast. It could be as high as ten seconds, I suppose. But let's aim for seven or eight as a good number. We'll have to position ourselves directly opposite the door so that the grenade concussion won't knock us off our feet. As soon as the door blows, we have to race across and through the opening."

"It shouldn't be hard to cross twenty meters in seven seconds," Larramac commented.

"Not under good circumstances, no. But all this junk on the ground makes the footing very treacherous. And we'll have to cut directly across the center of the shaft, which is the big danger zone. Plus," she added, shifting her weight to ease the pain in her left leg, "I can't move much faster than a hop any more."

"You can lean on my shoulder," Dunnis volunteered instantly. "If I could do it for Grgat I can do it for you."

"Thank you, Gros. Yes, we'll have to do it that way." She started limping around the perimeter of the shaft, then halted and conferred again. "We'll have even less time than I thought," she said. "In order to fire at the door, I'll have to turn on my headlamp again to aim properly. The robots will notice my lamp isn't near the ladder, and they'll take their clue from that. They must know we're near the bottom by now anyhow. So be prepared to move quickly."

She hobbled carefully around the rim, measuring off the distance she traveled and estimating it as a fraction of the total circumference. When she guessed she was halfway around she switched on her radio transmitter again and lifted her grenade launcher off her shoulders.

"Here goes," she said to warn her companions, and switched on her light.

She had gone slightly more than halfway around the circle, so she had to aim slightly back to her left. The brightness of her lamp dazzled her as it reflected off the metal surface of the wall ahead, but fortunately the grenade launcher did not require exact aiming to be effective. Squinting her eyes, she fired at the door.

The grenade hit and exploded with a satisfactory blast. This door was not as thick as the one in the mountain tunnel, and the force of the explosion shattered it. Small shards of metal flew through the air and light streamed out from the space beyond the door. Dev quickly slipped an arm through the launcher's shoulder strap and prepared to move.

"Let's go!" she yelled, but her words were unnecessary. Larramac had already started through the rain of metal across the shaft, and Dunnis was only waiting for her to get started before moving himself. Draping her left arm over the engineer's broad shoulders, Dev gave the signal she was ready.

The debris beneath them was uneven and shifted as they moved across it. Their gait was irregular, as they'd had no time to practice and co-ordinate their movements. More scrap metal rained down on them, striking the ground all around them with incredible force. Any one of those pieces would be lethal if it hit correctly.

Larramac had already made it through the door and the other two had only a few meters to go when they heard a whistling noise far above them. Whatever was coming, it was heavy and traveling at great speed. Before Dev could even react to the noise, Dunnis, whose arm was around her waist to steady her, spun her around and flung her bodily through the doorway. A bare instant later he had planted his own feet and leaped for the hole, diving out just before the cataclysm hit.

13

"To fail to accept the unalterable is insane; to fail to change the intolerable is criminal. You must train yourself to distinguish between them."

—Anthropos, *Sanity and Society*

There was a crash that resounded through the mountain as several tons of metal struck the ground at better than seventy kilometers a second. It sounded as though all the remaining robots had jumped off the edge of the shaft at once in a last, suicidal attempt to stop the humans. The clattering of metal was deafening— but the humans survived.

Dev landed on the ground on her left side and screamed with pain as her already injured leg suffered further abuse. She lay there for several minutes, eyes closed, oblivious to everything but the agony that was shooting through her foot.

Finally the pain subsided sufficiently for her to think of other things. They had made it through one more stage of the journey and survived another series of tests. If she hadn't known better, she would have thought this entire expedition a carefully designed sequence of tortures. She was dead tired, hungry, thirsty, and in a great deal of pain. Was it even worthwhile to go any further and suffer more torments?

Open your eyes, Dev, she told herself sternly. *Nobody's going to do it for you.*

She was panting heavily as she pried up her lids, but even so the sight she saw made her catch her breath. She was suddenly in a wonderland of pristine whiteness and restful pastels. The floor on which she lay, while covered with dust and shards of metal from the shattered door, was otherwise antiseptically clean. The walls sparkled brightly and the ceiling high above their heads was lost in the general diffuse glow of indirect lighting.

Slowly, doing her best to ignore the pain in her leg, she pulled herself into a sitting position and looked around. The two men were also staring silently about in disbelief. Apart from themselves, nothing moved; "sterile" was the word that popped first into Dev's mind.

"I don't know if we've died," she said, breaking the stillness, "but I think we've gone to Heaven."

Taking her rifle from her back she stood it on the ground and used it as a staff to pull herself to her feet. Once standing, she found she could use the weapon as a crutch; she felt awkward, but by no means helpless.

"You think the gods live here?" Dunnis asked.

"I don't think *anything* lives here," Dev replied. "This fanatical sterility seems incompatible with life. I've seen operating rooms dirtier than this." She shrugged. "Well, with all this cleanliness we must be right next to godliness."

A corridor stretched before them seemingly to infinity, all as white and pure as the section in which they stood. "Let's go down there and see what we can find," Larramac said, pointing into the distance.

Dev was so tired she could hardly see straight, and her left ankle was throbbing fiercely. But Larramac, for once, was right. All her intuition told her they were near the end of the journey. One way or another, this raid was going to be resolved, and it was better to have done with it all at once than drag it out still further. "Right," she nodded wearily.

They made a strange procession as the trio of humans marched down the sparkling hallway. Dunnis and Larramac, though not as seriously incapacitated as Dev, were every bit as tired, and their pace was more a stagger than a walk. Occasionally one or another of them would lean up against the wall for a momentary respite before continuing along the way. The walls felt cold, even through the insulated fabric of their suits.

Nowhere as they marched did they see anything to

165

break the absolute stillness around them. The feeling grew in Dev that she and the others were somehow desecrating a sepulcher. The walls on either side of them were unbroken, unseamed.

"We must be getting close," Larramac mused. "Why don't they try to stop us?"

"They don't dare," Dev said quietly. "There can be no violence here, no matter what the cost." She didn't know how she knew that, but it blazed like a fact in her mind that this level was somehow sacred, devoid of passion.

They'd gone more than three hundred meters before anything broke the monotony of the blank white walls. A large doorway stood on their left, three meters high and four wide. Beside the doorway, set into the wall, was a pink spot just below shoulder level. On impulse, Dev reached out with her hand and covered the spot with her palm; obediently, the double doors in front of them slid into the wall on either side.

They found themselves staring into a machine shop, fully equipped and completely automated. The trio stood on the threshold, afraid to enter, but Dunnis gave the shop a nod of approval. "With tools like these there's almost nothing I couldn't do," he whispered.

Dev, looking around, could only agree. "I'll keep that in mind."

Nowhere in the shop was there the faintest sign of life, so after a few minutes' gawking, Dev pulled them away from the scene. "We have gods to find, remember?"

They continued down the hallway for another two hundred meters before they found a second door. Again the portal slid open with a touch of the palm on a pressure-sensitive plate.

The area beyond the doors had been dark, but with the opening of the doors light sprang to life all over the chamber. They found themselves looking this time into a vast gray room, so big they couldn't begin to guess at its dimensions. And directly in front of them, settled securely on automated tracks, was something that could only be a starship.

It was nearly twice the size of *Foxfire* and its sleek,

streamlined shape was subtly different from any type of craft they'd seen before. It was old; the alien lettering on its hull was faded, and the walls were pitted and scarred from countless meteroid encounters—but it was a ship.

The same thought flashed through each of their minds. They all knew *Foxfire* would never take off again; it had dug its own grave in the mountainside. Each had secretly been hoping beyond hope they would make a discovery like this to get them home. Now their prayers had been answered.

They approached the ship cautiously. There was always the chance that it was still being used as headquarters by the gods, and they did not want to be caught off guard. Dev's left ankle was positively aflame with pain, but she would not stop now. She was the person who would best be able to assess the ship's capabilities, and she had to see it.

They had to walk around to the far side of the ship before they found the airlock. It was closed, which gave her a slight feeling of relief; she was wary of open invitations under circumstances like these—they could all too easily be traps. But, though this looked safer, there was still the problem of how to open the airlock.

Dunnis found the manual control box indented in the hull. There were instructions printed in an alien language, but the humans couldn't read them. The controls themselves were strange but not indecipherable. The engineer closed his eyes and let his hand wander over the surface of the instruments, trying to discover the most logical applications. After several trials he met with success. The hatch slid open with a sigh that whispered of long disuse.

The interior of the ship was dark, so they switched on their headlamps once again. Just past the airlock was a long corridor that ran fore to rear. They looked as far as their beams could penetrate in either direction, but saw no signs of life.

Dev made the decision to split up the party so they could search more effectively. She sent Dunnis down to the rear of the ship where the drive was most likely to be; he could tell from that whether the ship was still capable of flight. She and Larramac, meanwhile, continued forward to explore the less esoteric portions of the ship.

They found a series of tiny cubicles, each one barely big enough for a full-grown human, though possibly quite adequate for the original inhabitants. There were nearly a hundred of these cubicles, and Dev estimated they took up the vast majority of the ship's crew area.

Curious, she leaned inside one of the cells and looked around. Her headlamp showed her that the walls had been ripped out of the cubicle and that, behind the wall, there had been some sort of elaborate equipment. A few wires hung loose and disconnected, and several transparent plastic tubes no more than a centimeter in diameter lay literally rotting on the floor.

She looked into another cell, and saw the same sight. The ship was filled with row upon row of these empty, ripped-up cubicles. Her mind was fighting off its fatigue, working overtime to correlate this data with what they already knew.

Larramac, too, had been investigating the empty cells, and was looking at her now quite perplexed. "What do you make of it?" he asked.

"I'd guess this was a troop carrier. The actual flight crew needed would be small, with the 'cargo'—namely the fighters—stowed away in these cubicles."

"How could anyone live in so small an area?"

"Suspended animation of some sort. It makes a lot of sense, really. Freeze up your troops at your home base and thaw them out again when they reach the scene of battle in a month or so. They'd come out of the freezer all ready for action, without having the edge taken off them by enduring a long, boring flight. Also they wouldn't be using up nearly as huge a quantity of oxygen and food during the trip."

Larramac leaned against the back wall. He looked as though he wanted to stroke his beard, but that was impossible with his helmet on. "So a troop carrier from the losing side in a space war lands on an out-of-the-way planet like Dascham. Using their trained fighters and superior technology, they enslave the local people, build this entire mountain, and set themselves up as gods."

Dev nodded. "It makes a good working hypothesis, at least. Let's see what the rest of the ship is like."

They moved forward some more. They found the Commons area for the crew that actually ran the ship; it looked similar, in many respects, to comparable human facilities. Dev noted all of this with growing interest— but the big test would be the control room itself.

She had been very afraid she would find the control room in a shambles. It was obvious from the suspended animation cells that the gods had scavenged their ship to get the materials and equipment they needed. If the bridge had suffered a similar fate, their position would be hopeless. But when they came to that chamber it looked intact; they still had a chance to leave.

The setup she found was different from the standard human design, which was only to be expected. Instead of being aligned in a row, each ship's function had its own separate area and acceleration couch. Dev went immediately to the consoles and looked them over. At first glance they were hopelessly jumbled and incomprehensible, but as she continued to stare at them she let her eyes go slightly out of focus.

Patterns emerged, ones that looked achingly familiar. Dev grasped at them like the fading sensations of a just-ended dream, but they eluded her. Then her eyes came back into focus again and she was staring at a control board that was totally alien to her.

She looked up to see Larramac watching her. "What do you think?" he asked. "Can you make it work?"

"It'll take time, but—yes, I think I may be able to puzzle it out."

They walked back down the corridor and met Dunnis just inside the airlock. They quickly described their findings and asked how he had fared.

"The piles are dead," he said sadly.

"I expected that," Dev nodded. "All of Orrork was built around it, and then enough time had to elapse for the natives to forget the mountain was artificial. This ship has probably been here for thousands of years. The question is, though: can we reactivate it using what we have on hand?"

Dunnis closed his eyes and rubbed wearily at his forehead. "It'd be a project," he sighed. "Might take months, but—yeah, with that machine shop to help I suppose we could."

"You want to get home again, don't you?" Dev asked.

He grinned at her. "More than anything else in the Universe right now."

Clapping a friendly hand on his shoulder, she returned the grin. "Then I know we can do it." She turned around to include Larramac in her gaze. "Come on, let's get off the ship and see what the rest of heaven has to offer."

They went back out to the corridor of sparkling white and continued their slow progress down its length. All this time had elapsed and there had been no attempts made on their lives, no sign that the gods were even aware of them—or that the gods even existed. There was nothing but themselves to disturb the perfect stillness of this eerie Valhalla.

After several hundred more meters they came to another door. Rifles at the ready, they opened it and peered through. It was another room just as large, if not larger, than the one that held the starship. Enormous vats dominated the floor, with pipes running everywhere along the walls. Although the vats were long since dried out, there was still the scent of strange chemicals. Irregular stains on the floor indicated where spills had occurred ages before. The room felt as musty as the ship.

"What is it?" Larramac asked in a whisper.

"I've never seen anything like this," Dunnis admitted. His voice was no louder than his boss's.

"I have," Dev said, "but only in pictures. It was in a microspool I was reading one time about the planet Hellfire, where they manufacture the androids. This is an android-synthesizing plant."

They were silent for a moment, digesting that information. Everything up to this point had made sense, but this was unexpected. Then, quite suddenly, Larramac laughed. "The gods created the Daschamese in their own image?"

Dev nodded. "That has to be it. We thought they took over the native population and enslaved them. But if there was no native population, they'd have to create their own. It wouldn't take long—after ten or twenty years the androids would accelerate the process the natural way. Androids—at least human ones—are perfectly capable of biological reproduction on their own."

They fell silent once more as they looked around the vast chamber, letting their imaginations race back through the millennia to the time when this plant would be producing at full capacity.

It was Dunnis who first returned them to the present with the question that was high in all their minds. "But where are the gods themselves? They've got to be somewhere, don't they?"

"There's still the yellow brick road outside," Dev muttered.

"Huh?" Neither man caught her classical reference.

"I mean, let's travel down the corridor and see where it leads."

Again they set out walking, and again they encountered no signs of opposition. The blank walls slid past without a seam or sign of any further doorways, until at last they came to the very end of the hall. They faced one last door.

"Gentlemen," Dev said quietly, "I think we should prepare to meet, if not our Makers, then certainly the Makers of the Daschamese." She palmed the switch beside the portal and waited with rifle in hand as the door slid open into the side of the wall.

Before them stretched a double row of caskets. Each box was on a meter-high dais; the daises were spaced about a meter and a half apart, with a three-meter aisle between the two rows extending off into the distance. They couldn't count the total number of the boxes; the rows stretched on too far to estimate.

The voice that spoke suddenly in their ears startled them after the utter stillness that had prevailed until now. It seemed far too loud and quite mechanical. "Yes, you have found us. We are the gods of Dascham. We have infinite power over this world. We are immortal. We invite you to join us in our immortality."

"That's because they can't lick us," Dev muttered.

"If you refuse to accept our invitation," the voice went on, "you will be instantly dispatched. Even at this instant there are weapons of incalculable destruction aimed directly at you."

Dev walked confidently over to the nearest casket and sat down on top of it. "Let me see some of this 'incalculable destruction,'" she taunted. After a moment's pause, she smiled. "I thought as much. You've gotten so deeply into the habit of living that it's become an obsession. Thousands of years in semisuspension have given you a fear of death so deep no mortal could ever begin to understand it. You can't even allow yourselves to use weapons of *calculable* destruction near here; if you could, you wouldn't have let us get this far. You'd have struck us down the moment we entered the corridor at the far end. But you don't want violence even that close to you."

She got off the top of the coffin and examined it more closely. There seemed no way to pry it open, but there was a palm button on the side. She pressed it and the top changed from opaque to transparent. Dev stared at the contents for a moment, keeping her thoughts rigidly in tow to prevent reaction.

"Roscil, Gros, come here a moment," she called. "Come look upon the face of a god."

The other two came reluctantly, afraid of what they would see. There, inside the casket, was a white, almost formless lump of protoplasm that might once have been the body of a bearlike creature resembling the Daschamese. The skin was palid as a worm's, soft and watery as it lay in its bath of nutrient solutions. Clusters of wires and tubes connected it to the dais beneath the coffin. It was alive only by the grace of a liberal definition of the term. Its mental activity continued on in the collective consciousness of the gods, but its physical activity was nil. It would not have been able to move even had it wanted to.

The two men looked away, sickened to their stomachs. They'd not had any solid food in almost a full day, which was probably the only thing that kept them from vomiting.

"I don't think we're interested in your invitation," Dev told the gods.

There was a slight pause, and then the voice of the gods grew indignant and even louder. "Why did you choose to do this?" it asked. "We let you trade without interference. We never did you any harm."

"One of my crewmen might disagree with you, if you hadn't turned him into a small pile of cinders."

"He had to be destroyed. He broke the rules. The rules are necessary to maintain order. The rules cannot be violated."

"The rules are necessary only to prolong your own reign," Dev answered brusquely. "Order is maintained in any case by intelligent beings. It's specious to argue that any one set of rules is the only answer."

"Why did you come here?" the gods repeated.

Dev paused briefly to consider. The true reason, Larramac's greed, seemed rather paltry in view of all they had now undergone. Then, after the ship had crashed, simple survival had pressed them forward along this path. But that didn't sound like enough of a reason right now, either.

"Because you are not gods," she said at last, "and someone had to disabuse you of that notion sometime."

"WE ARE THE GODS OF DASCHAM!" the voice bellowed into their ears, making their heads ring. "Who are you to cast your judgment upon us?"

"My name is Ardeva Korrell," she said, "and I'm an intelligent, rational being. That gives me as much right as anybody."

Standing beside the case, she lifted her rifle and smashed the butt against the transparent top and sides. Liquid ran out onto the floor. The being

173

inside twitched several times before lying still.

For the next hour and a half, Dev and her companions walked down the rows of caskets, smashing them and destroying the feeble creatures within.

14

"The sane person knows how much responsibility he can handle and refuses to accept more."
—Anthropos, *The Sane Mind*

Because the gods had been unable to stir from their suspension chambers, their entire control over this vast computer complex had been run directly from their increasingly more senile brains. Air and light continued to be provided automatically, so Dev at long last agreed that they could remove their helmets; but killing the gods stopped the nonautomatic computer functions, which could cause potential problems.

The gods had not always been hooked directly into the computer, however. At the far end of the rows, after the last of the creatures had been destroyed, Dev found an enormous computer console, with diagrams laid out beside it for the master control of this entire mountain. The system was unfamiliar to her and her fatigue-fogged brain refused to work any further, so she called for a rest period before attempting to decipher this new mystery. "The danger is over," she announced. "Let's get some sleep and approach this problem fresh in a few hours."

It was actually closer to ten hours before she opened her eyes again. She had slept soundly despite the throbbing pain in her left ankle, which was now swollen up to immense proportions. Dev wished she could use the medchest aboard *Foxfire* when she got back to it, but she knew Bakori would be more in need of it than she was.

The thought of Bakori made her remember that he had been waiting back aboard ship for word from them. Putting her helmet back on, she switched the transmitting frequency to the main ship's circuit and started calling him. After ten minutes of steady signaling, he answered her.

The ship was still safe, he assured her. When the gods were destroyed the angels had fallen out of the sky; they now lay smashed and helpless on the ground around the base of the mountain. He himself was able to get around inside the ship by keeping himself doped up on painkillers, but he wanted her permission to use the medchest as soon as possible, before any permanent injury was done to his leg.

Dev told him to turn off the ship's drive, as it was no longer needed for protection. He was to remain out of the medchest for a little while longer—she would still need him as liaison with the ship until they established a new system.

Dunnis and Larramac were awake again by this time, and the three of them spent the next several hours trying to puzzle out the computer system the gods had used. It turned out to be an easier task than Dev had feared. She guessed that the numerical system would be based on eight, since that was the number of fingers the Daschamese had. Working from that point, decoding the computer language was largely a matter of trial and error. Also helping them was the fact that this computer was of the so-called co-operative style that worked with its programmer to achieve better results. All told, it took the three humans barely six hours to get into reasonable rapport with the machine that controlled Mount Orrork and, indirectly, all of Dascham.

There were still a good many robots functioning within the mountain including, Dev learned, three of the giant ones. There was also a series of exits scattered around the base of the mountain leading from the complex to the outside world, meaning that the humans would not have to retrace their torturous path to return to *Foxfire*.

Dev programmed the robots to obey all her orders and instructed the computer to run the entire Orrork complex through verbal commands whenever appropriate. With that giant step taken, events began proceeding in a speedy and orderly manner.

The humans returned triumphantly to their ship, accompanied by several robots. They ate a meal ravenously and then caught up on some more of their lost sleep. Then, with the help of the robots, they began transferring everything movable from *Foxfire* to the hangar where the gods' old spaceship was stored. The transferral was a week-long task, and Dev put Larramac in charge of that operation. She and Dunnis had other things to occupy their time.

The two ship's officers spent almost every waking hour inside the alien vessel, taking the walls apart, tracing every circuit, deducing how each control was intended to function. A starship is a complex mechanism, and they had no small task ahead of them. The Orrork computer was of some help by giving them blueprints and diagrams, but every single element had to be checked and rechecked to make certain it was still capable of functioning after all these millennia of disuse. In more than half the cases, repairs had to be made—and that took even more time and labor.

Bakori was finally allowed to use the medchest. He lay inside it, sedated, with tubes feeding him intravenously. An oxygen mask covered his face and his body floated in a sea of regenerative balm not unlike the substance that had been inside the gods' caskets. After diagnosing the severity of his leg injury, the medchest estimated his recovery time at two months. For that period, the astrogator would be in suspended animation and his services would be lost to the rest of them.

Dev's own ankle healed very slowly because she simply could not afford the time to rest and let it get better by itself. She was constantly up and working, moving around on an improvised crutch Dunnis had given her. She had to set the pace, she knew; the engineer was naturally a slow worker, and left to his own speed would never get the work done in time to do them any good.

They ate the food from *Foxfire*'s ample larder. The ship had been stocked for a five-month run with five people aboard. With only three people now using up the food, supplies could be expected to last a good deal longer. They were never rushed, but Dev refused to let the atmosphere drain of the tension and the need to work. As far as she was concerned, the sooner they were off this dismal world, the better.

After everything possible had been transferred to the new headquarters from *Foxfire,* Larramac found himself with time on his hands. He offered to help the other two, but he lacked the necessary technical knowledge of ship operations and often was more a hindrance than a help. Yet he was unpredictable enough that Dev was loathe to leave him to his own resources for fear of the trouble he might stir up.

Finally she hit on a plan to keep him busy. She suggested that he spend his time with the Orrork computer, interrogating it and discovering as much of the story as he could about the settling of Dascham. It was something they were all curious about, and it gave his sharp mind something to do. Larramac fell to his task with great enthusiasm, and they hardly ever saw him again except at mealtimes.

They renamed the alien ship *Foxfire II.* About three weeks after starting work on it, Dev and Dunnis made an interesting discovery—the ship was still armed with weapons that generated energy of the same kind as the angels, only on a much larger scale. They discussed their find at dinner that night with Larramac.

"No one I know has anything quite like that," the boss said eagerly. "We could sell that and make a fortune—or, better yet, hire some technicians to figure out how it works and manufacture it ourselves. We'll be rich a dozen times over."

"Perhaps," Dev said flatly. She remembered all too well the argument they'd had aboard *Foxfire* about selling weapons, and she still had scruples that would not permit her to get involved in anything of that order.

Larramac looked at her. He, too, remembered the argument. "Well, my little saint, what do *you* suggest we do with that lightning blaster?"

"For one thing, once this craft is safely launched I intend to use it to destroy Orrork."

Larramac was flabbergasted. "What in Space for?"

"As long as this complex is here, the possibility will remain for someone to take it over and become the new god. The Daschamese deserve better than that. They've been children long enough; they need the chance to grow up."

"But there's never been an installation of this size before. Think of its value just as a computing center alone."

"I have," Dev admitted. "It does have fantastic possibilities. But not here, where the people have no resistance to it. Let a computer mountain be built somewhere else, where it can be used properly and not turned automatically into an instrument of oppression."

The argument continued for a while longer, with neither side able to budge the other from its set stance. In the end, Larramac withdrew in a sulk and refused to speak to Dev for several days. That was all right with her; she had other work to do, anyway.

Days passed into weeks with astonishing speed. The ship's controls, which at first had seemed so confoundingly alien, were gradually becoming more and more familiar. Dev knew she would never be able to handle them at the instinctive speed with which she worked controls on a human-designed vessel, but she was daily gaining more confidence that she could lift the craft off the planet, slip it into hyperspace, and pilot it close enough to a human-inhabited world for them to be rescued. Using the records from *Foxfire,* she calculated that Windsong was the nearest available planet for their purposes. They would set a course for there.

With the problem of the controls all but licked, they turned their attention to the more basic question of the ship's dead power source. There was a fundamental difference between the way the gods had powered their craft and the method used by humans. Converting the latter to the former was a great deal harder than they originally thought. Dunnis had to make full use of the automated machine shop they'd discovered. Working in conjunction with the Orrork computer, he and Dev decided what mixture of the two systems would give optimum performance and how to go about producing the merger. The entire procedure took slightly over a month.

During that time, Larramac kept them well informed on his researches into Daschamese history. The picture that emerged fit within their rough outline, but with interesting details.

The initial settlers were a crew from a ship engaged on the losing side of a space war. Rather than die in hopeless battle, they mutinied and killed their captain, then took the ship to Dascham, a planet that supported life but had as yet developed no intelligent life forms. Not until the ship had landed did the crew wake their cargo of troopers—one at a time. Those soldiers who agreed to the defection joined the party; the few who remained loyal to their home planet and insisted on returning to duty were killed outright.

The first few years were hard, especially since the group consisted entirely of males. The idea of constructing androids was originally proposed as a method of obtaining some females to ease the hardships. None of the settlers was an expert on android development, but there was enough technical knowledge among them that, after years of trial and error, they were able to produce acceptable female androids. Once they proved they could do that, they started making other androids to work for them as servants.

The process quickly snowballed. With more labor available, production could be stepped up as well. Within several more years there were tens of thousands of androids, vastly outnumbering the original settlers, and yet made to work as slaves for their comfort.

Disaffection and discontent rose within the android ranks. At last they blossomed into a full-scale revolt, one that almost succeeded. The original soldiers were out of training and no longer young, but they did possess military knowledge that their slaves lacked. It was that knowledge alone that helped them crush the revolution—and the realization of how slender was the thread by which they lived startled them into more drastic action. They must above all protect their hegemony.

Their tyranny became harsher. They produced androids by the thousands, and robot overseers to keep them in line. They had the androids build the incredible fortress that, in the space of years, became Mount Orrork. Labor and materials were plentiful, time was not. The masters started using the suspended animation caskets scavenged from their ship and oversaw production in shifts; half of them would lie in stasis while the other half managed construction for a year, and then they would switch.

It took better than thirty years of continuous labor by hundreds of thousands of androids to build Orrork. There was no record of the deaths that occurred within that time, but the number must have been phenomenal. By that time, the original deserters, even with their one year on/one year off schedule, were getting old. They knew that, under normal circumstances, they would not long outlive their creation. And so they took the unprecedented step of establishing the system of perpetual suspended animation. Their bodies would lie in a bath of nutrient solution, being eternally cared for, while their brains would remain active. Linked into the computer, they would still be able to control the progress of life among their slaves. With the system of spying and terror that they imposed, they made Dascham into a theocracy that lasted for thousands of years—until increasing senility had taken the edge off their defenses and allowed the humans to penetrate and destroy them.

To Dev it sounded very tragic on all sides. It was tragic for the deserters, who were so trapped by their fear of death and their insecure compulsion to make themselves superior that they had to cut themselves off from direct corporeal experience. And it was tragic for generations of Daschamese, who grew up condemned to slavish existence, unable to develop or think for themselves.

As the day neared for their attempted departure,

Larramac became very moody, often not coming to meals with the rest of them. He started taking long solitary walks through the halls of this bottom floor of the mountain. Lian Bakori, though, came out of the medchest with his leg virtually healed. A small bit of work might be required by human surgeons, but he was free of pain and could move about as well as ever. Dev started him in immediately on a course of instruction to understand the alien astrogational equipment so he could plot their course back to Windsong. The hangar doors above the ship were opened wide, giving them a clear shot at the sky.

The night before they were to leave they were gathered together in the galley of *Foxfire II*. Larramac, as was happening more frequently, had not chosen to join them for the meal, but as they finished he came wandering in. Dev, with a sharp eye for detail, observed that his walk was a trifle too casual—calculatedly so.

She also noticed another detail—Larramac was wearing his pistol in the holster at his belt. None of the rest of them was armed.

"I've been doing some thinking," the boss said. "So far this entire trip has turned out to be a loss, financially speaking. I think I've come up with a way to salvage a good profit out of it."

Dev did not think this was the moment to remind him that she had predicted the disaster. She and the others waited to hear his idea.

"Grgat promised us a reward to help him defeat the gods. Well, unfortunately he died in the attempt, but we succeeded in doing what he asked. That means the natives are morally obligated to pay us back for our services."

"Moral obligations are the hardest to collect," Dev said quietly.

"Not in this case. We've still got a lot of the gods' apparatus intact. The natives don't have to know there's been a change in management. We can have them pay their tribute to us."

"In other words," Dunnis said slowly, "you're suggesting that we take the gods' place and enslave these people."

"Well, that's putting it crudely. I'd just suggest we let them work off their debt. We *did* go through an awful lot, all for their sakes. We can rebuild the angels . . ."

"Didn't you see what the gods looked like?" Dev asked. "Do you want to turn into something like that?"

Larramac shook his head. "It wouldn't be that way. I wouldn't make their mistake of trying to go on forever. There are too many things I like to do to be cooped up here on this planet for a thousand years. I was just thinking of five years or so. We have the entire population and resources of this world at our disposal. In five years, we could amass enough wealth to live comfortably back in civilization for the rest of our lives. Just imagine all you could do with what we'd take home."

"And what about the Daschamese?" Dev asked. "The whole point of this exercise was to gain them their freedom. When do they get that?"

"Well, they won't be any worse off than they were before we came, will they? They can have their freedom five years from now, after they've paid us off."

"What's to keep you from extending that for just one more year, and then another and another? Power can be addictive, Roscil; it's better not to get hooked on the habit in the first place."

Larramac snorted. "You're a fine one to talk. All you Eoans think you're gods anyway."

"I'm a god to myself, but you won't find me trying to extend my jurisdiction. If you rule someone else, you become responsible for him, and I have enough responsibilities without accepting any more."

Larramac looked around him. Bakori was a null; he would accept in his own quiet fashion any decision that was made. Dev was being quietly hostile, and he could guess she would never side with him in this scheme. Dunnis was looking dubious. More and more, the engineer was tending to side with Dev against his employer.

Larramac played his last card. "I'm your boss," he said, "and you'll do what I tell you."

Dev shook her head. "You're the owner of *Foxfire* and

you paid us to run it for you. *Foxfire* is now deceased, and we're in a lifeboat situation. No one is anybody's boss except for me. As captain, emergency regulations give me extraordinary powers in a situation like this, and my word is law."

Dev had been keeping a careful watch on Larramac's right hand as it moved closer to the butt of his pistol, but even so the situation exploded faster than she had expected. As *Foxfire*'s owner reached for his weapon, she pushed her chair back quickly from the table and stood up. There was perhaps a meter and a half of distance between her and Larramac, and she would have to cover it before he could do any damage.

Her bad leg hampered her. The ankle had healed by itself and she was now able to get around quite well under ordinary circumstances. But putting sudden weight on it and expecting it to function quickly sent a sharp stabbing pain through her left leg. She stumbled as she rose from the table, but managed to lurch forward into Larramac.

Her attack was quick enough to deflect his aim, and the laser bolt zipped cleanly through the table top without hitting anyone. The weight of her body falling against his knocked him off balance and he went backward against the wall.

Dunnis had been startled by the sudden gunplay, but recovered his wits faster than Dev would have expected. He rushed to her aid and grabbed at Larramac's gun hand, wresting the object away by sheer force.

Larramac was snarling with rage at being thwarted. Lashing out with his foot, he kicked the engineer squarely in the belly, sending the bigger man backward across the room with the wind knocked out of him. Dev was fighting to grab hold of Larramac, but he pushed her away from him into Bakori's lap. Then, spinning around, Larramac raced out of the galley and down the corridor to the outside hatch.

Dev picked herself up and ran after him but, with her sore leg, she was no match for the man. By the time she made it to the ship's airlock Larramac was halfway across the open floor of the hangar, running to the control room of the main computer.

Dev watched him run and said a private good-by to him. Then she turned back and returned to the galley. There was work to be done—quickly.

"Get up into the control room," she said to the two startled men. "We have to take off now, this instant, or we'll never get another chance!"

Dunnis was just getting to his feet, still a bit stunned by the kick. "Why not?"

Dev helped him up and guided him in the right direction. "Don't you see, he can't let us get away without him. If we should return to another human planet and tell our tale, somebody else might get the same idea as Roscil's. They could come in with a whole army to take over his mountain, and there's not much he could do to stop them. The only way he can ensure his safety is to keep us from leaving."

"But how can he do that? We have the ship and most of the weapons are stored below." They had made it onto the bridge now, and were busy strapping themselves into the acceleration couches at their stations.

Dev pointed at a viewscreen that showed the scene directly above them. The overhead doors they had opened several days ago still gaped widely at the sky—but for how long?

"He's been working with the computer more closely than the rest of us. If he orders it to shut those doors before we can get outside, we'll either smash ourselves against the metal or else never get off the ground. We can't give him that opportunity—the way he is now he'd kill us before letting us go. Give me internal artigrav, now!"

"Without even a preflight checkout?"

"Have you been listening to a word I've said? If we wait for the niceties we'll never leave."

"I don't have a course set," Bakori said.

"I'll forgive you this once," Dev told him. "Let's just get out of this hole and we'll worry about where we're headed later."

Dunnis was going through the motions of activating

185

the proper controls with agonizing slowness as he dealt under stress with the unfamiliar console. Dev was laboring under the same conditions, and found herself sweating profusely. It seemed as though all the learning she had done in the past two months wanted to erase itself from her mind, leaving her staring at the alien controls dumbfoundedly. She fought that feeling, making herself go by rote over her panel, ticking off what each switch did.

The internal artificial gravity came on quite suddenly, startling her out of her trance. "All set at my end," Dunnis said. "It's in your lap now, Captain."

Dev reached out and touched the appropriate controls. The entire ship trembled as it woke abruptly from its millennia-long nap and tried to yank itself to instant action. Without the preflight checkout the systems were sluggish, reluctant to respond to her commands. In a couple of instances, Dev had to switch power off and then on again before achieving the proper effect.

They could feel no motion as the ship began to rise from the floor where it had lain dormant so long, but on the viewscreen they could see the sky jumping toward them. Just as they started moving, Dev, who'd kept one eye glued to the screen, saw the large overhead doors start to slide themselves together. Throwing all caution to the winds, she switched instantly to full power, willing to tax the untested engines to the limit in her effort to get them free of Orrork.

The internal gravity field shot up suddenly to nearly four g's as the ship leaped into the rapidly closing breach. Dev could tell from looking at the screen that they'd make it at least partway out—but whether the doors would snap shut on them as they exited would be a matter decided by only a few seconds.

She closed her eyes and fought against the heavy acceleration, bracing herself for the loud clang and the shock of the doors crunching on the ship's hull. But the battering never came and, after ten uneventful seconds had passed, Dev dared open her eyes again.

The ship was free, pulling rapidly away from the

mountain into the skies. Dev reached out a hand and dropped the power levels back until their acceleration was down to a less-than-orbital one and a fraction pg's. "Gros," she asked, "is the system stable enough to hold us in place here for a couple of minutes?"

"I suppose so. Why?"

Dev didn't answer directly. She stabilized their position and played with the viewscreen until Mount Orrork came into view once more about three kilometers below them. When she determined they were righted enough to hold their position for at least a short while, she unstrapped herself from her couch and walked across the control room to the gunner's console.

Dunnis watched her in horror as the realization of what she was going to do slowly came to him. "You can't," he said. "Roscil's down there!"

"That was a choice he made voluntarily," Dev said. Her words were clipped and brisk, her tone cold. "We cannot leave him down there in control of that computer."

"Why not? He can't hurt us now."

"But there are millions of Daschamese whom he can hurt—and he will, in his present mental condition." Her voice softened as she turned to look Dunnis directly in the eyes. "I don't like the thought of killing him, either. He was a friend through some hard times, and he hired me when no one else would. But the man who did those things no longer exists. If I let him live, I will be responsible—if only indirectly—for the pain and suffering of millions of intelligent beings. That is something I, for one, do not choose to live with."

Dunnis said nothing. He knew that what his captain said was true—Larramac would take out his rage and frustrations on the natives, who could not fight back. There was also in his mind the knowledge that Larramac had tried to kill them to prevent them from leaving—and would try again if given the chance.

With a tear in his eye he flipped three necessary switches. "Power to the gunner's console," he said hoarsely.

Dev continued to look at him even after he averted his gaze. "Thank you, Gros," she said quietly.

Turning, then, she primed her generators and took aim on Mount Orrork. Her manner was all business. She thought of the mountain as a target only, and refused even to consider the human life that existed within it. Without the slightest sign of hesitation, she fired.

Bolts of incredible energy lanced downward through the atmosphere. They struck the mountainside with explosions that shook the ground for hundreds of kilometers around. The hillside ripped open, exposing to view the naked machinery of the mountain's interior.

Dev fired again, and more explosions tore at the gods' former stronghold. Smoke billowed up from the ruined edifice in thick white clouds that momentarily obscured Dev's view. When the clouds passed, she fired a third time and now the superstructure of the mountain itself collapsed. Tons of material caved inward and the entire landscape was choked with the dust raised by the implosion.

"I think that will do it," she announced. "The bottom levels may have survived, and Roscil with them—but even if they did, there's nothing he can do alone to rebuild Orrork. He'll have to take his chances as a mortal, the same as everyone else."

She walked slowly back to her own acceleration couch.

"It would probably be best, when we get back to our own civilization, if we lie a little about what happened here. What I said a little while ago about having emergency powers in this situation is perfectly true—but if some smart prosecutor tries to build up a case of mutiny against us, he could conceivably damage our reputations and make it even harder for us to get work." Dev shivered as she realized she was unemployed again. "We could have to fight a long, costly legal battle to justify our actions. I don't think any of us wants that. Let's just say Roscil died while fighting with the gods. In part, that's true."

"And what about the natives?" Dunnis asked. "What happens to them now that the gods are gone?"

"Well, they don't know that right now, so for a while

they'll probably go right on with their normal routine. It may take them months or years to realize the extent of their freedom—perhaps even centuries. They'll never completely erase the influence the gods had on their mentality and culture, just as humanity's never been able to wipe out our own beginnings. We use it as a base from which to grow—and I'm sure they'll do the same."

She turned to Bakori. "Astrogator, plot us a course for Windsong. I want to get out of here as soon as possible."

And as *Foxfire II* departed the atmosphere of Dasçham forever, it left behind a world that had yet to realize it was awakening.

Bestselling SF/Horror

☐ The Labyrinth	Robert Faulcon	£2.50
☐ Night Train	Thomas F. Monteleone	£2.50
☐ Doomflight	Guy N. Smith	£2.50
☐ Malleus Maleficarum	Montague Summers	£4.95
☐ The Devil Rides Out	Dennis Wheatley	£2.95
☐ Cities in Flight	James Blish	£2.95
☐ Stand on Zanzibar	John Brunner	£2.95
☐ 2001 – A Space Odyssey	Arthur C. Clarke	£1.95
☐ Gene Wolfe's Book of Days	Gene Wolfe	£2.25
☐ The Shadow of the Torturer	Gene Wolfe	£2.50
☐ The Blackcollar	Timothy Zahn	£1.95
☐ Speaker for the Dead	Orson Scott Card	£2.95
☐ The War for Eternity	Christopher Rowley	£2.95
☐ Contact	Carl Sagan	£3.50

Prices and other details are liable to change

ARROW BOOKS, BOOKSERVICE BY POST, PO BOX 29, DOUGLAS, ISLE OF MAN, BRITISH ISLES

NAME ....

ADDRESS ....

....

....

Please enclose a cheque or postal order made out to Arrow Books Ltd. for the amount due and allow the following for postage and packing.

U.K. CUSTOMERS: Please allow 22p per book to a maximum of £3.00.

B.F.P.O. & EIRE: Please allow 22p per book to a maximum of £3.00.

OVERSEAS CUSTOMERS: Please allow 22p per book.

Whilst every effort is made to keep prices low it is sometimes necessary to increase cover prices at short notice. Arrow Books reserve the right to show new retail prices on covers which may differ from those previously advertised in the text or elsewhere.